TREK THROUGH TIME!

There was the sensation, indescribable, but which he had told me was not quite unlike swimming against a high tide. The sun rose in the west and skidded eastward; then, as he "accelerated," light became a vague pulsation of grayness, and everywhere around him reached shadow. It was altogether silent.

He glimpsed a shellburst—soundless, misty—but was at once past the Six Day War, or had that been the War of Independence or the First World War? Wan shapes drifted past.

On a cloudy night in the late nineteenth century he must reenter normal time for air. . . .

Tor books by Poul Anderson

Alight in the Void
The Armies of Elfland
The Boat of a Million Years
The Dancer from Atlantis
Explorations
Harvest of Stars
Hoka! (with Gordon R. Dickson)
Kinship with the Stars
A Knight of Ghosts and Shadows
The Long Night
The Longest Voyage
A Midsummer Tempest
No Truce with Kings
Past Times
The Saturn Game
The Shield of Time
Tales of the Flying Mountains
The Time Patrol

THERE WILL BE TIME

POUL ANDERSON

A TOM DOHERTY ASSOCIATES BOOK
NEW YORK

THERE WILL BE TIME

Cover art by Duane Meyers

A Tor Book
Published by Tom Doherty Associates, Inc.
175 Fifth Avenue
New York, N.Y. 10010

Tor® is a registered trademark of Tom Doherty Associates, Inc.

ISBN: 0-812-52308-3

First Tor mass market edition: October 1993

Printed in the United States of America

0 9 8 7 6 5 4 3 2 1

foreword

Be at ease. I'm not about to pretend this story is true. First, that claim is a literary convention which went out with Theodore Roosevelt of happy memory. Second, you wouldn't believe it. Third, any tale signed with my name must stand or fall as entertainment; I am a writer, not a cultist. Fourth, it *is* my own composition. Where doubts or gaps occur in that mass of notes, clippings, photographs, and recollections of words spoken which was bequeathed me, I have supplied conjectures. Names, places, and incidents have been changed as seemed needful. Throughout, my narrative uses the techniques of fiction.

Finally, I don't believe a line of it myself. Oh, we could get together, you and I, and ransack official files, old newspapers, yearbooks, journals, and so on forever. But the effort and expense would be large; the results, even if positive, would prove little; we have more urgent jobs at hand; our discoveries could conceivably endanger us.

These pages are merely for the purpose of saying a little about Dr. Robert Anderson. I do owe the book to him. Many of the sentences are his, and my aim throughout has been to capture something of his style and spirit, in memoriam.

You see, I already owed him much more. In what follows, you may recognize certain things from earlier stories of mine. He gave me those ideas, those backgrounds and people, in hour after hour while we sat with sherry and Mozart before a driftwood fire, which is the best kind. I greatly modified them, in part for literary purposes, in part to make the tales my own work. But the core remained his. He would accept no share of payment. "If you sell it," he laughed, "take Karen out to an extravagant dinner in San Francisco, and empty a pony of akvavit for me."

Of course, we talked about everything else too. My memories are rich with our conversations. He had a pawky sense of humor. The chances are overwhelming that, in leaving me a boxful of material in the form he did, he was turning his private fantasies into a final, gentle joke.

On the other hand, parts of it are uncharacteristically bleak.

Or are they? A few times, when I chanced to be present with one or two of his smaller grandchildren, I'd notice his pleasure in their company interrupted by moments of what looked like pain. And when last I saw him, our talk turned on the probable shape of the future, and suddenly he exclaimed, "Oh, God, the young, the poor young! Poul, my generation and yours have had it outrageously easy. All we ever had to do was be white Americans in reasonable health, and we got our place in the sun. But now history's returning to its normal climate here also, and the norm is an ice age." He tossed off his glass and poured a refill more quickly than was his wont. "The tough and lucky will survive," he said. "The rest . . . will have had what happiness was granted them. A medical man ought to be used to that kind of truth, right?" And he changed the subject.

In his later years Robert Anderson was tall and spare, a bit stoop-shouldered but in excellent shape, which he attributed to hiking and bicycling. His face was likewise lean, eyes blue behind heavy glasses, clothes and white hair equally rumpled. His speech was slow, punctuated by gestures of a pipe if he was enjoying his twice-a-day smoke. His manner was relaxed and amiable. Nevertheless, he was as independent as his cat. "At my stage of life," he observed, "what was earlier called oddness or orneriness counts as lovable eccentricity. I take full advantage of the fact." He grinned. "Come your turn, remember what I've said."

On the surface, his life had been calm. He was born in Philadelphia in 1895, a distant relative of my father. Though our family is of Scandinavian origin, a branch has been in the States since the Civil War. But he and I never heard of each other till one of his sons, who happened to be interested in genealogy, happened to settle down near me and got in touch. When the old man came visiting, my wife and I were invited over and at once hit it off with him.

His own father was a journalist, who in 1910 got the editorship of the newspaper in a small upper-midwestern town (current population 10,000; less then) which I choose to call Senlac. He later described the household as nominally Episcopalian and principally Democratic. He had just finished his premedical studies when America entered the First World War and he found himself in the Army; but he never got overseas. Discharged, he went on to his doctorate and internship. My impression is that meanwhile he exploded a bit, in those hip-flask days. It cannot have been too violent. Eventually he returned to Senlac, hung out his shingle, and married his longtime fiancée.

I think he was always restless. However, the work of general practitioners was far from dull—before progress condemned them to do little more than man referral desks—and his marriage was happy. Of four children, three boys lived to adulthood and are still flourishing.

In 1955 he retired to travel with his wife. I met him soon afterward. She died in 1958 and he sold their house but bought a cottage nearby. Now his journeys were less extensive; he remarked quietly that without Kate they were less fun. Yet he kept a lively interest in life.

He told me of those folk whom I, not he, have called the Maurai, as if it were a fable which he had invented but lacked the skill to make into a story. Some ten years later he seemed worried about me, for no reason I could see, and I in my turn worried about what time might be doing to him. But presently he came out of this. Though now and then an underlying grimness showed through, he was mostly himself again. There is no doubt that he knew what he was doing, for good or ill, when he wrote the clause into his will concerning me.

I was to use what he left me as I saw fit.

Late last year, unexpectedly and asleep, Robert Anderson took his death. We miss him.

chapter 1

The beginning shapes the end, but I can say almost nothing of Jack Havig's origins, despite the fact that I brought him into the world. On a cold February morning, 1933, who thought of genetic codes, or of Einstein's work as anything that could ever descend from its mathematical Olympus to dwell among men, or of the strength in lands we supposed were safely conquered? I do remember what a slow and difficult birth he had. It was Eleanor Havig's first, and she quite young and small. I felt reluctant to do a Caesarian; maybe it's my fault that she never conceived again by the same husband. Finally the red wrinkled animal dangled safe in my grasp. I slapped his bottom to make him draw his indignant breath, he let the air back out in a wail, and everything proceeded as usual.

Delivery was on the top floor, the third, of our county hospital, which stood at what was then the edge of town. Removing my surgical garb, I had a broad view out a window. To my right, Senlac clustered along a frozen river, red brick at the middle, frame homes on tree-lined streets, grain elevator and water tank rearing ghostly in dawnlight near the railway station. Ahead and to my left, hills rolled wide and white under a low gray sky, here and there roughened by leafless woodlots, fence lines, and a couple of farmsteads. On the edge of sight loomed a darkness which was Morgan Woods. My breath misted the pane, whose chill made my sweaty body shiver a bit.

"Well," I said half aloud, "welcome to Earth, John Franklin Havig." His father had insisted on having names ready for either sex. "Hope you enjoy yourself."

Hell of a time to arrive, I thought. A worldwide depression hanging heavy as winter heaven. Last year noteworthy for the Japanese conquest of Manchuria, bonus march on Washington, Lindbergh kidnapping. This year begun in the same style: Adolf Hitler had become Chancellor of Germany. . . . Well, a new President was due to enter the White House, the end of Prohibition looked certain, and springtime in these parts is as lovely as our autumn.

I sought the waiting room. Thomas Havig climbed to his feet. He was not a demonstrative man, but the question trembled on his lips. I took his hand and beamed. "Congratulations, Tom," I said. "You're the father of a bouncing baby boy. I know—I just dribbled him all the way down the hall to the nursery."

My attempt at a joke came back to me several months afterward.

Senlac is a commercial center for an agricultural area; it maintains some light industry, and that's about the list. Having no real choice in the matter, I was a Rotarian, but found excuses to minimize my activity and stay out of the lodges. Don't get me wrong. These people are mine. I like and in many ways admire them. They're the salt of the earth. It's simply that I want other condiments too.

Under such circumstances, Kate's and my friends tended to be few but close. There was her banker father, who'd staked me; I used to kid him that he'd done so because he wanted a Democrat to argue with. There was the lady who ran our public library. There were three or four professors and their wives at Holberg College, though the forty miles between us and them was considered rather an obstacle in those days. And there were the Havigs.

These were transplanted New Englanders, always a bit homesick; but in the '30's you took what jobs were to be had. He taught physics and chemistry at our high school. In addition, he must coach for track. Slim, sharp-featured, the shyness of youth upon him as well as an inborn reserve, Tom got through his secondary chore mainly on student tolerance. They were fond of him; besides, we had a good football team. Eleanor was darker, vivacious, an avid tennis player and active in her church's poor-relief work. "It's fascinating, and I think it's useful," she told me early in our acquaintance. With a shrug: "At least it lets Tom and me feel we aren't altogether hypocrites. You may've guessed we only belong because the school board would never keep on a teacher who didn't."

I was surprised at the near hysteria in her voice when she phoned my office and begged me to come.

A doctor's headquarters were different then from today, especially in a provincial town. I'd converted two front rooms of the big old house where we lived, one for interviews, one for examination and treatments, including minor surgery. I was my own receptionist and secretary. Kate helped with paperwork—looking back from now, it seems impossibly little, but perhaps she never let on—and, what few times patients must wait their turns, she entertained them in the parlor. I'd made my morning rounds, and nobody was due for a while; I could jump straight into the Marmon and drive down Union Street to Elm.

I remember the day was furnace-hot, never a cloud above or a breath below, the trees along my way standing like cast green iron. Dogs and children panted in their shade. No birdsong broke the growl of my car engine. Dread closed on me. Eleanor had cried her Johnny's name, and this was polio weather.

But when I entered the fan-whirring venetian-blinded dimness of her house, she embraced me and shivered. "Am I going crazy, Bob?" she gasped, over and over. "Tell me I'm not going crazy!"

"Whoa, whoa, whoa," I murmured. "Have you called Tom?" He eked out his meager pay with a summer job, quality control at the creamery.

"No, I . . . I thought—"

"Sit down, Ellie." I disengaged us. "You look sane enough to me. Maybe you've let the heat get you. Relax—flop loose—unclench your teeth, roll your head around. Feel better? Okay, now tell me what you think happened."

"Johnny. Two of him. Then one again." She choked. "The *other* one!"

"Huh? Whoa, I said, Ellie. Let's take this a piece at a time."

Her eyes pleaded while she stumbled through the story. "I, I, I was bathing him when I heard a baby scream. I thought that must be from a buggy or something, outside. But it sounded as if it came from the . . . the bedroom. At last I wrapped Johnny in a towel—I couldn't leave him in the water—and carried him along for a, a look. And there was another tiny boy, there in his crib, naked and wet, kicking and yelling. I was so astonished I . . . dropped mine. I was bent over the crib, he should've landed on the mattress, but, oh, Bob, he didn't. He vanished. In midair. I'd made a, an instinctive grab for him. All I caught was the towel. Johnny was gone! I think I must've passed out for a few seconds. And when I hunted I—found—nothing—"

"What about the strange baby?" I demanded.

"He's . . . not gone . . . I think."

"Come on," I said. "Let's go see."

And in the room, immensely relieved, I crowed: "Why, nobody here but good ol' John."

She clutched my arm. "He looks the same." The infant had calmed and was gurgling. "He sounds the same. Except he can't be!"

"The dickens he can't. Ellie, you had a hallucination. No great surprise in this weather, when you're still weak." Actually, I'd never encountered such a case before, certainly not in a woman as levelheaded as she. But my words were not too implausible. Besides, half a GP's medical kit is his confident tone of voice.

She wasn't fully reassured till we got the birth certificate and compared the prints of hands and feet thereon with the child's. I prescribed a tonic, jollied her over a cup of coffee, and returned to work.

When nothing similar happened for a while, I pretty well forgot the incident. That was the year when the only daughter Kate and I would ever have caught pneumonia and died, soon after her second birthday.

Johnny Havig was bright, imaginative, and a loner. The more he came into command of limbs and language, the less he was inclined to join his peers. He seemed happiest at his miniature desk drawing pictures, or in the yard modeling clay animals, or sailing a toy boat along the riverbank when an adult took him there. Eleanor worried about him. Tom didn't. "I was the same," he would say. "It makes for an odd childhood and a terrible adolescence, but I wonder if it doesn't pay off when you're grown."

"We've got to keep a closer eye on him," she declared. "You don't realize how often he disappears. Oh, sure, a game for him, hide-and-seek in the shrubbery or the basement or wherever. Grand sport, listening to Mommy hunt up the close and down the stair, hollering. Someday, though, he'll find his way past the picket fence and—" Her fingers drew into fists. "He could get run over."

The crisis came when he was four. By then he understood that vanishing meant spankings, and had stopped (as far as his parents knew. They didn't see what went on in his room). But one summer morning he was not in his bed, and he was not to be found, and every policeman and most of the neighborhood were out in search.

At midnight the doorbell rang. Eleanor was asleep, after I had commanded her to take a pill. Tom sat awake, alone. He dropped his cigarette—the scorch mark in the rug would long remind him of his agony—and knocked over a chair on his way to the front entrance.

A man stood on the porch. He wore a topcoat and shadowing hat which turned him featureless. Not that that made any difference. Tom's whole being torrented over the boy who held the man by the hand.

"Good evening, sir," said a pleasant voice. "I believe you're looking for this young gentlemen?"

And, when Tom knelt to seize his son, hold him, weep and try to babbly thanks, the man departed.

"Funny," Tom said to me afterward. "I couldn't have been focusing entirely on Johnny for more than a minute. You know Elm Street has good lamps and no cover. Even in a sprint, nobody could get out of sight fast. Besides, running feet would've set a dozen dogs barking. But the pavement was empty."

The child would say nothing except that he had been "around," and was sorry, and wouldn't wander again.

Nor did he. In fact, he emerged from his solitariness to the extent of acquiring one inseparable friend, the Dunbar boy. Pete fairly hulked over his slight, quiet companion. He was no fool; today he manages the local A & P. But John, as he now wanted to be called, altogether dominated the relationship. They played his games, went to his favorite vacant lots and, later, his chosen parts of Morgan Woods, enacted the histories of his visionary worlds.

His mother sighed, in my cluttered carbolic-and-leather-smelling office: "I suppose John's so good at daydreaming that even for Pete, the real world seems pale by contrast. That's the trouble. He's too good at it."

This was in the second year following. I'd seen him through a couple of the usual ailments, but otherwise had no cause to suspect problems and was startled when Eleanor requested an appointment to discuss him. She'd laughed over the phone: "Well, you know Tom's Yankee conscience. He'd never let me ask you professional questions on a social occasion." The sound had been forlorn.

I settled back in my creaky swivel chair, bridged my fingers, and said, "Do you mean he tells you things that can't be true, but which he seems to believe are? Quite common. Always outgrown."

"I wonder, Bob." She frowned at her lap. "Isn't he kind of old for that?"

"Perhaps. Especially in view of his remarkably fast physical and mental development, these past months. However, practicing medicine has driven into my bones the fact that 'average' and 'normal' do not mean the same. . . . Okay. John has imaginary playmates?"

She tried to smile. "Well, an imaginary uncle."

I lifted my brows. "Indeed? Just what has he said to you?"

"Hardly anything. What do children ever tell their parents? But I've overheard him talking to Pete, often, about his Uncle Jack who comes and takes him on all sorts of marvelous trips."

"Uncle Jack, eh? What kind of trips? To this kingdom you once mentioned he's invented, which Leo the Lion rules over?"

"N-no. That's another weird part. He'll describe Animal Land to Tom and me; he knows perfectly well it's pure fantasy. But these journeys with his 'uncle' . . . they're different. What snatches I've caught are, well, realistic. A visit to an Indian camp, for instance. They weren't storybook or movie Indians. He described work they had to do, and the smell of drying hides and dung fires. Or, another time, he claimed he'd been taken on an airplane ride. I can see how he might dream up an airplane bigger than a house. But why did he dwell on its having no propellers? I thought boys loved to go *eee-yowww* like a diving plane. No, his flew smooth and nearly noiseless. A movie was shown aboard. In Technicolor. He actually had a name for the machine. Jet? Yes, I think he said 'jet.' "

"You're afraid his imagination may overcome him?" I asked needlessly. When she nodded, swallowing, I leaned forward, patted her hand, and told her:

"Ellie, imagination is the most precious thing childhood has got. The ability to imagine in detail, like those Indians, is beyond valuation. Your boy is more than sane; he may be a genius. Whatever you do, never try to kill that in him."

I still believe I was right—totally mistaken, but right.

On this warm day, I chuckled and finished, "As for his, uh, jet airplane, I'll bet you a dozen doughnut holes Pete Dunbar has a few Buck Rogers Big Little Books."

All small boys were required to loathe school, and John went through the motions. No doubt much of it did bore him, as must be true of any kid who can think and is forced into lockstep. However, his grades were excellent, and he was genuinely gripped by what science and history were offered. ("A star passed near our sun and pulled out a ribbon of flaming gas that became the planets. . . . The periods of world civilization are Egypt, Greece, Rome, the Middle Ages, and modern time, which began in 1492.")

His circle of friends, if not intimates, widened. Both sets of parents regretted that my Billy was four years older, Jimmy two and Stuart three years younger, than Johnny. At their stage of life, those gaps dwarfed the Grand Canyon. John shunned organized games, and by and large existed on the fringes of the tribe. For instance, Eleanor had to do the entire organizing of his birthday parties. Nevertheless, between his gentle manner and his remarkable fund of conversation—when someone else took the initiative and stimulated him—he was fairly well liked.

In his eighth year he caused a new sensation. A couple of older boys from the tough side of the tracks decided it would be fun to lie in wait for individuals on their way back from school and pummel them. Buses only carried farm children, and Senlac wasn't yet built solid; most walking routes had lonely spots. Naturally, the victims could never bring themselves to complain.

The sportsmen did, after they jumped John Havig. They blubbered that he'd called an army to his aid. And beyond doubt, they had taken a systematic drubbing.

The tale earned them an extra punishment. "Bullies are always cowards," said fathers to their sons. "Look what happened when that nice Havig boy stood up and fought." For a while he was regarded with awe, though he blushed and stammered and refused to give details; and thereafter we called him Jack.

Otherwise the incident soon dropped into obscurity. That was the year when France fell.

"Any news of the phantom uncle?" I asked Eleanor. Some families had gotten together for a party, but I wanted a respite from political talk.

"What?" She blinked, there where we stood on the

Stocktons' screened porch. Lighted windows and buzzing conversation at our backs didn't blot out a full moon above the chapel of Holberg College, or the sound of crickets through a warm and green-odorous dark. "Oh." She dimpled. "You mean my son's. No, not for quite a while. You were right, that was only a phase."

"Or else he's learned discretion." I wouldn't have uttered my thought aloud if I'd been thinking.

Stricken, she said, "You mean he may have clammed up completely? He is reserved, he does tell us nothing important, or anybody else as far as I can learn—"

"I.e.," I said in haste, "he takes after his dad. Well, Ellie, you got yourself a good man, and your daughter-in-law will too. Come on, let's go in and refresh our drinks."

My records tell me the exact day when, for a while, Jack Havig's control broke apart.

Tuesday, April 14, 1942. The day before, Tom had made the proud announcement to his son. He had not mentioned his hope earlier, save to his wife, because he wasn't sure what would happen. But now he had the notice. The school had accepted his resignation, and the Army his enlistment, as of term's end.

Doubtless he could have gotten a deferment. He was over thirty, and a teacher, of science at that. In truth, he would have served his country better by staying. But the crusade had been preached, the wild geese were flying, the widowmaker whistled beyond the safe dull thresholds of Senlac. I also, middle-aged, looked into the possibility of uniform, but they talked me out of trying.

Eleanor's call drew me from bed before sunrise. "Bob, you've got to come, right away, please, please. Johnny. He's hysterical. Worse than hysterical. I'm afraid . . . brain fever or—Bob, come!"

I hurried to hold the thin body in my arms, try to make

sense of his ravings, eventually give him an injection. Before then Jack had shrieked, vomited, clung to his father like a second skin, clawed himself till blood ran and beaten his head against the wall. "Daddy, Daddy, don't go, they'll kill you, I know, I know, I saw, I was there an' I saw, I looked in that window right there an' Mother was crying, Daddy, Daddy, Daddy!"

I kept him under graduated sedation for the better part of a week. That long was needed to quiet him down. He was a listless invalid until well into May.

This was absolutely no normal reaction. Other boys whose fathers were off to war gloried, or claimed they did. Well, I thought, Jack wasn't any of them.

He recovered and buckled down to his schoolwork. He was in Tom's company at every imaginable opportunity, and some that nobody would have imagined beforehand. This included furloughs, spent at home. Between times, he wrote almost daily letters to his father—

—who was killed in Italy, August 6, 1943.

chapter 2

A doctor cannot endure having made his inevitable grisly blunders unless he recalls enough rescues to offset them. I count Jack Havig among those who redeemed me. Yet I helped less as a physician than as a man.

My special knowledge did let me see that, beneath a tight-held face, the boy was seriously disturbed. Outside the eastern states, gasoline was not rationed in 1942. I arranged for a colleague to take over my practice, and when school closed, Bill and I went on a trip . . . and we took Jack along.

In Minnesota's Arrowhead we rented a canoe and entered that wilderness of lakes, bogs, and splendid timber which reaches on into Canada. For an entire month we were myself, my thirteen-year-old son, and my all but adopted son whom I believed to be nine years of age.

It's rain and mosquito country; paddling against a headwind is stiff work; so it portaging; to make camp required more effort than if we'd had today's ingenious gear and freeze-dried rations. Jack needed those obstacles, that nightly exhaustion. After fewer days than might have been awaited, the land could begin to heal him.

Hushed sunrises, light gold in the uppermost leaves and ashiver across broad waters; birdsong, rustle of wind, scent of evergreen; a squirrel coaxed to take food from a hand; the soaring departure of deer; blueberries in a bright warm opening of forest, till a bear arrived and we most respectfully turned the place over to him; moose, gigantic and unafraid, watching us glide by; sunsets which shone through the translucent wings of bats; dusk, fire and stories and Bill's young wonderings about things, which showed Jack better than I could have told him how big a world lies beyond our sorrows; a sleeping bag, and stars uncountable.

It was the foundation of a cure.

Back home again, I made a mistake. "I hope you're over this notion about your father, Jack. There's no such thing as foreknowing the future." He whitened, whirled, and ran from me. I needed weeks to regain his confidence.

His trust, at any rate. He confided nothing to me except the thoughts, hopes, problems of an ordinary boy. I spoke no further of his obsession, nor did he. But as much as time and circumstance allowed, I tried to be a little of what he so desperately lacked, his father.

We could take no more long excursions while the war lasted. However, we had country roads to tramp, Morgan Woods to roam and picnic in, the river for fishing and swimming, Lake Winnego and my small sailboat not far off. He could come around to my garage workshop and make a bird feeder for himself or a broom rack for his mother. We could talk.

I do believe he won to a measure of calm about Tom's death by the time it happened. Everybody assumed his premonition was coincidental.

Eleanor had already taken a job in the library, plus giving quite a few hours per week to the hospital. Widowhood struck her hard. She rallied gamely, but for a long while was subdued and unsocial. Kate and I tried to get her out, but she declined invitations more often than not.

When at last she began to leave her shell, it was mostly in the company of others than her old circle. I couldn't keep from remarking: "You know, Ellie, I'm damn glad to see you back in circulation. Still—forgive me—your new friends are kind of a surprise."

She reddened and looked away. "True," she said low.

"Perfectly good people, of course. But, uh, not what you'd call intellectual types, are they?"

"N-no. . . . All right." She straightened in her chair. "Bob, let's be frank. I don't want to leave here, if only because of what you are to Jack. Nor do I want to be buried alive, the way I was that first couple of years. Tom influenced me; I don't really have an academic turn of mind like his. And . . . you who we went with . . . you're all married."

I abandoned as useless my intention in raising the matter—to tell her how alien her son was to those practical-minded, loud-laughing men who squired her around, how deeply he was coming to detest them.

He was twelve when the nuclear thunderbolts slew two cities and man's last innocence. Though the astonishing growth rate I had noted in him earlier had slowed down to average since 1942, its effect remained to make him precocious. That reinforced the extreme solitariness which had set in. No longer was Pete Dunbar, or any schoolmate, more than a casual associate. Politely but unshakably, Jack refused everything extracurricular. He did his lessons, and did them well, but his free time was his and nobody else's: his to read enormously, with emphasis on history books; to take miles-long hikes by himself; to draw pictures or to shape things with the tools I'd helped him collect.

I don't mean he was morbid. Lonely boys are not uncommon, and generally become reasonably sociable adults. Jack was fond of the Amos 'n' Andy program, for instance, though he preferred Fred Allen; and he had a dry wit of his own. I remember various of his cartoons he showed me, one in particular suggested by a copy of *The Outsider and Others* which I lent him. In a dark, dank forest were two human figures. The first, cowering and pointing, was unmistakably H. P. Lovecraft. His companion was a tweedy woman who snapped: "Of course they're pallid and mushroomlike, Howard. They *are* mushrooms."

While he no longer depended on me, we saw a good bit of each other; and the age difference between him and Bill was less important now, so that they two sometimes went together for a walk or a swim or a boat ride—even, in 1948, a return to northern Minnesota with Jim and Stuart.

Soon after he came back from this, my second son asked me: "Daddy, what's a good book on, uh, philosophy?"

"Eh?" I laid down my newspaper. "Philosophy, at thirteen?"

"Why not?" Kate said across her embroidery. "In Athens he'd have started younger."

"Well, m-m, philosophy's a mighty wide field, Jim," I stalled. "What's your immediate question?"

"Oh," he mumbled, "free will and time and all that jazz. Jack Havig and Bill talked a lot about it on our trip."

I learned that Bill, being in college, had begun by posing as an authority, but soon found himself entangled in problems—was the history of the universe written before its beginning? if so, why do we know we make free choices? if not, how can we affect the course of the future . . . or the past?—which it didn't seem a high school kid could have pondered as thoroughly as Jack had done.

When I asked my protégé what he wanted for Christmas, he answered: "Something I can understand that explains relativity."

In 1949, Eleanor remarried. Her choice was catastrophic.

Sven Birkelund meant well. His parents had brought him from Norway when he was three; he was now forty, a successful farmer in possession of a large estate and fine house ten miles outside town, a combat veteran, and a recent widower who had two boys to raise: Sven, Jr., sixteen, and Harold, nine. Huge, red-haired, gusty, he blazed forth maleness—admitted Kate to me, though she couldn't stand him—and he was not unlettered either; he subscribed to magazines (*Reader's Digest*, *National Geographic*, *Country Gentlemen*), read an occasional book, liked travel, and was a shrewd businessman.

And . . . Eleanor, always full of life, had been celibate for six years.

You can't warn someone who's tumbled into love. Neither Kate nor I tried. We attended the wedding and reception and offered our best wishes. Mostly I was conscious of Jack. The boy had grown haggard; he moved and talked like a robot.

In his new home, he rarely got a chance to see us. Afterward he would not go into detail about the months which followed. Nor shall I. But consider: Where Eleanor was a dropout from the Episcopal Church, and Jack a born agnostic, Birkelund was a Bible-believing Lutheran. Where Eleanor enjoyed gourmet cooking and Jack the eating, Birkelund and his sons wanted meat and potatoes. Tom spent his typical evening first with a book, later talking with her. If Birkelund wasn't doing the accounts, he was glued to the radio or, presently, the television screen. Tom had made a political liberal of her. Birkelund was an ardent and active American Legionnaire—he never missed a convention, and if you draw the obvious inference, you're right—who became an outspoken supporter of Senator Joseph McCarthy.

And on and on. I don't mean that she was disillusioned overnight. I'm sure Birkelund tried to please her, and gradually dropped the effort only because it was failing. The fact that she was soon pregnant must have forged a bond between then which lasted a while. (She told me, however, I being the family doctor, that in the later stages his nightly attentions became distasteful but he wouldn't stop. I called him in for a Dutch-uncle lecture and he made a sulky compromise.)

For Jack the situation was hell from the word go. His stepbrothers, duplicates of their father, resented his invasion. Junior, whose current interests were hunting and girls, called him a sissy because he didn't like to kill and a queer because he never dated. Harold found the numberless ways to torment him which a small boy can use on a bigger one whose fists may not defend.

More withdrawn than ever, he endured. I wondered how.

In the fall of 1950, Ingeborg was born. Birkelund named her after an aunt because his mother happened to be called Olga. He expressed disappointment that she was a girl, but threw a large and drunken party anyway, at which he repeatedly declared, amidst general laughter, his intention of trying for a son the minute the doctor allowed.

The doctor and his wife had been invited, but discovered a prior commitment. Thus I didn't see, I heard, how Jack walked out on the celebration and how indignant Birkelund was. Long afterward, Jack told: "He cornered me in the barn when the last guest had left who wasn't asleep on the floor, and said he was going to beat the shit out of me. I told him if he tried, I'd kill him. I meant that. He saw it, and went off growling. From then on, we spoke no more than we could avoid. I did my chores, my share of work come harvest or whatever, and when I'd eaten dinner I went to my room."

And elsewhere.

The balance held till early December. What tipped it doesn't matter—something was bound to—but was, in fact, Eleanor's asking Jack if he'd given thought to the college he would like to attend, and Birkelund shouting, "He can damn well get the lead out and go serve his country like I did and take his GI if they haven't cashiered him," and a quarrel which sent her upstairs fleeing and in tears.

Next day Jack was not there.

He returned at the end of January, would say no word about where he had been or what he had done, and stated that he would leave for good if his stepfather took the affair to the juvenile authorities as threatened. I'm certain he dominated that scene, and won himself the right to be left in peace. Both his appearance and his demeanor were shockingly changed.

Again the household knew a shaky equilibrium. But six weeks later, upon a Sunday when Jack had gone for his usual long walk after returning from church, he forgot to lock the door to his room. Little Harold noticed, entered, and rummaged through the desk. His find, which he promptly brought to his father, blew apart the whole miserable works.

Snow fell, a slow thick whiteness filling the windows. What daylight seeped through was silver-gray. Outdoors the air felt almost warm—and how utterly silent.

Eleanor sat on our living-room couch and wept. "Bob, you've got to talk to him, you, you've got to help him . . . again . . . What happened when he ran away? What did he *do*?"

Kate laid arms around her and drew the weary head down to her own shoulder. "Nothing wrong, my dear," she murmured. "Oh, be very sure. Always remember, Jack is Tom's son."

I paced the rug, in the dull twilight against which we had turned on no lights. "Let's spell out the facts," I said, speaking bolder than I felt. "Jack had this mimeographed pamphlet that Sven describes as Communist propaganda. Sven wants to call the sheriff, the district attorney, anybody who can force Jack to tell who he fell in with while he was gone. You slipped out to the shed, drove off in the pickup, met the boy on the road, and brought him here."

"Y-y-yes. Bob, I can't stay. Ingeborg's at home. . . . Sven will call me an, an unnatural mother—"

"I might have a few words to say about privacy," I answered, "not to mention freedom of speech, press, and opinion." After a pause: "Uh, you told me you snaffled the pamphlet?"

"I—" Eleanor drew back from Kate's embrace. Through tears and hiccoughs, a strength spoke that I remembered: "No use for him to call copper if the evidence is gone."

"May I see it?" I asked.

She hesitated. "It's . . . a prank, Bob. Nothing s-s-significant. Jack's waiting—"

—in my office, by request, while we conferred. He had shown me a self-possession which chilled this winter day.

"He and I will have a talk," I said, "while Kate gets some coffee, and I expect some food, into you. But I've got to have something to talk about."

She gulped, nodded, fumbled in her purse, and handed me several sheets stapled together. I settled into my favorite armchair, left shank on right knee, a good head of steam in my pipe, and read the document.

I read it twice. And thrice. I quite forgot the women.

Here it is. You won't find any riddles.

But hark back. The date was the eleventh of March, in the year of Our Lord nineteen hundred and fifty-one.

Harry S Truman was President of the United States, having defeated Thomas E. Dewey for election, plus a former Vice President who would later have the manhood to admit that his party had been a glove on the hand of Moscow. This was the capital of a Soviet Union which my adored FDR had assured me was a town-meeting democracy, our gallant ally in a holy war to bring perpetual peace. Eastern Europe and China were down the gullet. Citizens in the news included Alger Hiss, Owen Lattimore, Judith Coplon, Morton Sobell, Julius and Ethel Rosenberg. Somehow, to my friends and myself, they did not make Joseph McCarthy less of an abomination. But under the UN flag, American young men were dying in battle—five and a half years after our V-days!—and their killers were North Korean and Chinese. Less than two years ago, the first Russian atomic bombs had roared. NATO, hardly older, was a piece of string in the path of hundreds of divisions. Most of us, in an emotional paralysis which let us continue our daily lives, expected World War III to break out at any instant.

I could not altogether blame Sven Birkelund for jumping to conclusions.

But as I read, and read, my puzzlement deepened.

Whoever wrote this thing knew Communist language—I'd been through some books on that subject—but was emphatically not a Communist himself. What, then, was he?

Hark back, I say. Try to understand your world of 1951.

Apart from a few extremists, America had never thought to question her own rightness, let alone her right to exist. We knew we had problems, but assumed we could solve them, given time and good will, and eventually everybody of every race, color, and creed would live side by side in the suburbs and sing folk songs together. *Brown vs. Board of Education* was years in the future; student riots happened in foreign countries, while ours worried about student apathy; Indochina was a place where the French were experiencing vaguely noticed difficulties.

Television was hustling in, and we discussed its possible effects. Nuclear-armed intercontinental missiles were on their way, but nobody imagined they could be used for anything except the crudest exchange of destructions. Overpopulation was in the news but would soon be forgotten. Penicillin and DDT were unqualified friends of man. Conservation meant preserving certain areas in their natural states and, if you were sophisticated about such matters, contour plowing on hillsides. Smog was in Los Angeles and occasionally London. The ocean, immortal mother of all, would forever receive and cleanse our wastes. Space flight was for the next century, when an eccentric millionaire might finance a project. Computers were few, large, expensive, and covered with blinking lights. If you followed the science news, you knew a little about transistors, and perhaps looked forward to seeing cheap, pocket-sized radios in the hands of Americans; they could make no difference to a peasant in India or Africa. All contraceptives were essentially mechanical. The gene was a locus on the chromosome. Unless he blasted himself back to the Stone Age, man was committed to the machine.

Put yourself in 1951, if you can, if you dare, and read as I did that jape on the first page of which appeared the notice "Copyright © 1970 by John F. Havig."

chapter 3

WITHIT'S COLLEGIATE DICTIONARY

Activist: a person employing tactics in the cause of *liberation* which, when used by a *fascist*, are known as *McCarthyism* and *repression.*
Aggression: Any foreign policy advocated by a *fascist.*

Black: Of whole or partial sub-Saharan African descent; from the skin color, which ranges from brown to ivory. Not to be confused with *Brown*, *Red*, *White*, or *Yellow*. This word replaces the former "Negro," which today is considered insulting since it means "Black."
Bombing: A method of warfare which delivers high explosives from the air, condemned because of its effects upon women, children, the aged, the sick, and other noncombatants, unless these happen to have resided in Berlin, Hamburg, Dresden, Tokyo, Osaka, etc., though not Hiroshima or Nagasaki. Cf. *missile*.
Brown: Of Mexican descent; from the skin color, which ranges from brown to ivory. Not to be confused with *Black*, *Red*, *White*, or *Yellow.*

Brutality: Any action taken by a policeman: Cf. *pig.*

Chauvinism: Belief of any Western *White* man that there is anything to be said for his country, civilization, race, sex, or self. *Chauvinist:* Any such man; hence, by extension, a *fascist* of any nationality, race, or sex.

Colonialist: Anyone who believes that any European- or North American-descended person has any right to remain in any territory outside Europe or North America where his ancestors happened to settle, unless these were Russian. Cf. *native.*

Concentration camp: An enclosed area into which *people* suspect to their government or to an occupying power are herded. No *progressive* country or *liberation* movement can operate a concentration camp, since by definition these have the full support of the *people.* NB: Liberals consider it impolite to mention Nisei in this connection.

Conformist: One who accepts *establishment* values without asking troublesome questions. Cf. *nonconformist.*

Conservative: See *aggression, bombing, brutality, chauvinism, colonialist, concentration camp, conformist, establishment, fascist, imperialist, McCarthyism, mercenary, military-industrial complex, missile, napalm, pig, plutocrat, prejudice, property rights, racist, reactionary, repression, storm trooper, xenophobia.*

Criminal: A *fascist,* especially when apprehended and punished. Cf. *martyr.*

Democracy: A nation in which the government, freely elected, remains responsive to the popular will, e.g., Czechoslovakia.

Development: (1) In *fascist* countries, the bulldozing of trees and hillsides, erection of sleazy row houses, etc., or in general, the exploitation of the environment. (2) In *progressive* countries, the provision of housing for the masses, or in general, the utilization of natural resources to satisfy human needs.

Ecology: (1) Obsolete: The study of the interrelationships of living things with each other and with the general environment. (2) Everything nonhuman which is being harmed by the *establishment*, such as trees and falcons but not including rats, sparrows, algae, etc. Thus *progressive* countries have no ecology.

Establishment: The powers that be, when these are *conservative.*

Fallout: Radioactive material from a *nuclear weapon*, widely distributed if this is tested in the atmosphere, universally condemned for its deleterious effect upon public health and heredity, unless the test is conducted by a *progressive* country.

Fascist: A person who favors measures possibly conducive to the survival of the West.

Freedom: Instant gratification.

Glory: An outworn shibboleth, except when applied to a *hero* or *martyr.*

Hero: A person who sacrifices and takes risks in a *progressive* cause. Cf. *pig* and *storm trooper.*

Honor: See *glory.*

Human rights: All rights of the *people* to *freedom*, when held to take infinite precedence over *property rights*, since the latter are not human rights.

Imperialist: A person who advocates that any Western country retain any of its overseas territory.

* * *

Liberation: Foreign expulsion and domestic overthrow of Western governments, influences, and institutions. *Sacred liberation:* Liberation intended to result in a (*People's*) *Republic.*
Love: An emotion which, if universally felt, would automatically solve all human problems, but which some (see *conservative*) are by definition incapable of feeling.

Martyr: A person who suffers or dies in the cause of *liberation.* Not to be confused with a *criminal* or, collectively, with enemy *personnel.*
McCarthyism: Character assassination for political purposes, by asserting that some person is a member of the Communist conspiracy, especially when this is done by an admirer of Sen. Joseph McCarthy. Not to be confused with asserting that some person is a member of the *fascist* conspiracy, especially when this is done by an admirer of Sen. Eugene McCarthy.
Mercenary: A soldier who, for pay, serves a government not his own. Cf. *United Nations.*
Military-industrial complex: An interlocking directorate of military and industrial leaders, held to be in effective control of the USA. Not to be confused with military and industrial leaders of the USSR or the various (*People's*) *Republics.*
Missile: A self-contained device which delivers high explosives from the air, condemned for its effects upon women, children, the aged, the sick, and other noncombatants, unless these happen to have resided in Saigon, Da Nang, Hué, etc. Cf. *bombing.*

Napalm: Jellied gasoline, ignited and propelled against enemy *personnel*, condemned by all true liberals except when used by Israelis upon Arabs.
Native: A non-*White* inhabitant of a region whose ancestors dispossessed the previous lot.

Nonconformist: One who accepts *progressive* values without asking troublesome questions. Cf. *conformist.*
Nuclear weapon: A weapon employing some form of atomic energy, used by *fascist* governments for purposes of *aggression* and by *progressive* governments to further the cause of *peace.*

One man, one vote: A legal doctrine requiring that, from time to time, old gerrymanders be replaced with new ones. The object of this is the achievement of genuine *democracy.*
Organic: Of foods, grown only with natural manures, etc., and with no chemical sprays, etc., hence free of harmful residues and of earthborne diseases or serious insect infestation, since surrounding lands have been artificially fertilized and chemically sprayed.

Peace: The final solution of the *fascist* problem. *Peaceful coexistence:* A stage preliminary to *peace* in which *aggression* is phased out and *sacred liberation* proceeds.
People: (Always used with the definite article and often capitalized.) Those who support *liberation.* Hence everyone not a *fascist* is counted among them, whether he wants to be or not.
Personnel: Members of a military or police organization, whether hostile or useful. Not to be confused with human beings.
Pig: (1) An animal known for its value, intelligence, courage, self-reliance, kindly disposition, loyalty, and (if allowed to follow its natural bent) cleanliness. (2) A policeman. Cf. *activist.*
Plutocrat: A citizen of a *republic* who, because of enormous wealth which he refuses to share with the *poor*, wields undue political power. Not to be confused with a Kennedy.

Poor: (Always used with the definite article and often capitalized.) That class of persons who are defined by someone as possessing less than their rightful wealth and privilege. The *progressive* definition includes all non-*fascist Black*, *Brown*, *Red*, and *Yellow* persons, regardless of income.

Pot: Marijuana. Must we go through that alcohol-tobacco-tranquilizers-are-legal routine again?

Prejudice: Hostility or contempt for a person or group, on a purely class basis and regardless of facts. Not to be confused with judgment passed on enemies of the *people* (see *conservative*).

Progressive: Conducive to *liberation*.

Property rights: The alleged rights of persons who have earned or otherwise lawfully obtained property, or of taxpayers who have similarly acquired property which is then designated public, to be secure in the enjoyment thereof, irrespective of *human rights*.

Racist: A *White* person who, when any *Black* person rings a bell, fails to salivate.

Reactionary: Not *progressive*.

Red: (1) Of American Indian descent; from the skin color, which ranges from brown to ivory. Not to be confused with *Black*, *Brown*, *White*, or *Yellow*, nor with "Mexican," even though most Mexicans are of American Indian stock. (2) Struggling for *liberation* or struggling in its aftermath.

Repression: Denial of the right of free speech, e.g., by refusal to provide a free rostrum for an *activist*, or the right of a free press, e.g., by refusing to print, televise, or stock in libraries every word of an *activist*, or the right to be heard, e.g., by mob action against an *activist*. Not to be confused with protection of the *people* from *reactionary* infection.

Republic: A country whose government is chosen not on

a basis of heredity or riches but by the electorate, from whom political power grows. *People's Republic:* One in which the electorate consists of a gun barrel.

Self-determination: The right of a culturally or ethnically distinct group to govern themselves, as in Biafra, East Pakistan, Goa, Katanga, the Sinai, Tibet, the Ukraine, etc.
Storm trooper: A person who sacrifices and takes risks in a *fascist* cause. Cf. *hero.*

United Nations: An international organization which employs Swedish, Indian, Irish, Canadian, etc. troops in other parts of the world than these so as to further *self-determination.*

White: Of Caucasoid descent; from the skin color, which ranges from brown to ivory. Not to be confused with *Black, Brown, Red,* or *Yellow.*
Winds of change: Poetic metaphor for the defeat of *reactionary* forces. Not applicable to any advance or restoration of these.
Women's Liberation: A movement which opposes male *chauvinism.*

Xenophobia: Distrust of the ability of strangers to run your life for you.

Yellow: Of Mongoloid descent; from the skin color, which ranges from brown to ivory. Not to be confused with *Black, Brown, Red,* or *White.*

chapter 4

For a moment, as I entered, my office was foreign to me. That rolltop desk, gooseneck reading lamp, worn leather-upholstered swivel chair and horsehair-stuffed seat for visitors, shelf of reference books, framed diploma, door ajar on the surgery to give a glimpse of cabinets wherein lay instruments and drugs that Koch would mostly have recognized—all was out of place, a tiny island in time which the ocean was swiftly eroding away; and I knew that inside of ten years I'd do best to retire.

The snowfall had thickened, making the windows a pale dusk. Jack had turned the lamp on so he could read a magazine. Beyond its puddle of light, shadows lay enormous. The steam radiator grumbled. It turned the air dry as well as warm.

He rose. "Sorry to give you this bother, Dr. Anderson," he said.

I waved him back into the armchair, settled myself down, reached for a fresh pipe off the rack. That much smoking was hard on the mouth, but my fingers needed something to do.

Jack nodded at the pamphlet I'd tossed on the desk. "How do you like it?" he asked tonelessly.

I peered through the upper half of my bifocals. This was not the boy who knew he would lose his father, nor the youth who tried and failed to hide his wretchedness when his mother took upon him a stepfather—only last year. A young man confronted me, whose eyes were old.

They were gray, those eyes, in a narrow straight-nosed face upon a long head. The dark-blond hair, the slim, middle-sized, slightly awkward body were Tom's; the mouth, its fullness and mobility out of place in that ascetic countenance, was Eleanor's; the whole was entirely Jack Havig, whom I had never fathomed.

Always a careless dresser, he wore the plaid wool shirt and blue denims in which he had gone for that tramp across the hills. His attitude seemed alert rather than uneasy, and his gaze did not waver from mine.

"Well," I said, "it's original. But you must admit it's sort of confusing." I loaded the pipe.

"Yeah, I suppose. A souvenir. I probably shouldn't have brought anything back."

"From your, uh, trip away from home? Where were you, Jack?"

"Around."

I remembered a small stubborn person who gave the same reply, after an unknown had returned him to his father. It led me to recall much else.

My wooden match made a *scrit* and flare which seemed unnaturally strong. I got the tobacco burning, took a good taste and smell of it, before I had my speech put together.

"Listen, Jack. You're in trouble. Worse, your mother is." That jarred him. "I'm the friend of you both, I want to help, but damnation, you'll have to cooperate."

"Doc, I wish I could," he whispered.

I tapped the pamphlet. "Okay," I said, "tell me you're

working on a science-fiction story or something, laid in 1970, and this is background material. Fine. I'd think you're needlessly obscure, but never mind; your business." Gesturing with the pipestem: "What is not your business is the fact it's mimeographed. Nobody mimeographs anything for strictly personal use. Organizations do. What organization is this?"

"None. A few friends." His neck stiffened. "Mighty few, among all those Gadarene swine happily squealing their slogans."

I stood. "How about a drink?"

Now he smiled. "Thanks. The exact prescription I want."

Pouring from a brandy bottle—sometimes it was needful for both a patient and myself, when I must pronounce sentence—I wondered what had triggered my impulse. Kids don't booze, except a little beer on the sly. Do they? It came to me afresh, here was no longer a kid.

He drank in the way of an experienced if not heavy drinker. How had he learned? He'd been gone barely a month.

I sat again and said: "I don't ask for secrets, Jack, though you know I hear a lot in my line of work, and keep them. I *demand* your help in constructing a story, and laying out a program of future behavior, which will get your mother off the hook."

He frowned. "You're right. The trouble is, I can't think what to tell you."

"The truth, maybe?"

"Doc, you don't want that. Believe me, you don't."

" 'Beauty is truth, truth beauty—' Why did Keats hand the world that particular piece of BS? He'd studied medicine; he knew better. Jack, I'll bet you ten dollars I can relate a dozen true stories which'll shock you worse than you could ever shock me."

"I won't bet," he said harshly. "It wouldn't be fair to you."

I waited.

He tossed off his drink and held out the glass. In the yellow lamplight, gaunt against the winter window, his face congealed with resolution. "Give me a refill, please," he said, "and I will tell you."

"Great." The bottle shook a bit in my grasp as the liquor clucked forth. "I swear to respect any confidentiality."

He laughed, a rattling noise. "No need for oaths, Doc. You'll keep quiet."

I waited.

He sipped, stared past me, and murmured: "I'm glad. It's been such a burden, through my whole life, never to share the . . . the fact of what I am."

I streamed smoke from my lips and waited.

He said in a rush, "For the most part I was in the San Francisco area, especially Berkeley. For more than a year."

My fingers clenched on the pipe bowl.

"Uh-huh." He nodded. "I came home after a month's absence. But I'd spent about eighteen months away. From the fall of 1969 to the end of 1970."

After a moment, he added: "That's not a whole year and a half. But you've got to count my visits to the further future."

Steam hissed in the radiator. I saw a sheen of sweat on the forehead of my all but adopted son. He gripped his tumbler as tightly as I my pipe. Yet in spite of the tension in him, his voice remained level.

"You have a time machine?" I breathed.

He shook his head. "No. I move around in time by myself. Don't ask me how. I don't know."

His smile jerked forth. "Sure, Doc," he said. "Paranoia. The delusion that I'm something special in the cosmos. Okay, I'll give you a demonstration." He waved about.

"Come here, please. Check. Make certain I've put no mirrors, trapdoors, gimmickry in your own familiar office."

Numbly, I felt around him, though it was obvious he'd had no chance to bring along, or rig, any apparatus.

"Satisfied?" he asked. "Well, I'll project myself into the future. How far? Half an hour? No, too long for you to sit here gnawing your pipe. Fifteen minutes, then." He checked his watch against my wall clock. "It's 4:17, agreed? I'll reappear at 4:30, plus or minus a few seconds." Word by word: "Just make sure nobody or nothing occupies this chair at that period. I can't emerge in the same space as another solid body."

I stood back and trembled. "Go ahead, Jack," I said through the thuttering in my veins.

Tenderness touched him. He reached to squeeze my hand. "Good old Doc. So long."

And he was gone. I heard a muted *whoosh* of air rushing in where he had sat, and nothing else. The chair stood empty. I felt, and no form occupied it.

I sat down once more at my desk, and stared for a quarter of an hour which I don't quite remember.

Abruptly, there he was, seated as he had been.

I struggled not to faint. He hurried to me. "Doc, here, take it easy, everything's okay, here, have a drink—"

Later he gave me a one-minute show, stepping back from that near a future to stand beside himself, until the first body vanished.

Night gathered.

"No, I don't know how it works," he said. "But then, I don't know how my muscles work, not in the way you know—and you'll agree your scientific information is only a glimmer on the surface of a mystery."

"How does it feel?" I asked, and noticed in surprise the calm which had come upon me. I'd been stunned longer on Hiroshima Day. Well, maybe the bottom of my mind had already guessed what Jack Havig was.

"Hard to describe." He frowned into darkness. "I . . . will myself backward or forward in time . . . the way I will to, oh, pick my glass off your desk. In other words, I order whatever-it-is to move me, the same as we order our fingers to do something, and it happens."

He searched for words before he went on: "I'm in a shadow world while I time-travel. Lighting varies from zero to gray. If I'm crossing more than one day-and-night period, it flickers. Objects look dim, foggy, flat. Then I decide to stop, and I stop, and I'm back in normal time and solidness. . . . No air reaches me on my way. I have to hold my breath, and emerge occasionally for a lungful if the trip takes that long in my personal time."

"Wait," I said. "If you can't breathe en route, can't touch anything or be touched, can't be seen—how come you have the feeble vision you do? How can light affect you?"

"I don't know either, Doc. I've read physics texts, however, trying to get a notion about that as well as everything else. And, oh, it must be some kind of force which moves me. A force operating in at least four dimensions, nevertheless a force. If it has an electromagnetic component, I can imagine how a few photons might get caught in the field of it and carried along. Matter, even ionized matter, has rest mass and therefore can't be affected in this fashion. . . . That's a layman's guess. I wish I dared bring a real scientist in on this."

"Your guess is too deep for me already, friend. Uh, you said a crossing isn't instantaneous, as far as you yourself are concerned. How long does it take? How many minutes per year, or whatever?"

"No particular relationship. Depends on me. I feel the effort I'm exerting, and can gauge it roughly. By, well, straining, I can move . . . faster . . . than otherwise. That leaves me exhausted, which seems to me to prove that time-traveling uses body energy to generate and apply the thrusting force. . . . It's never taken more than a few minutes, according to my watch; and that was a trip through several centuries."

"When you were a baby—" My voice halted.

He nodded anew. "Yeah, I've heard about the incident. Fear of falling's an instinct, isn't it? I suppose when my mother dropped me, I threw myself into the past by sheer reflex . . . and thereby caused her to drop me."

He took a swallow of brandy. "My ability grew as I grew. I probably have no limit now, if I can stop at need, along the way, to rest. But I am limited in the mass I can carry along. That's only a few pounds, including clothes. More, and I can't move; it's like being weighted down. If you grabbed me, for instance, I'd be stuck in normal time till you let go, because you're too much for me to haul. I couldn't just leave you behind; the force acts, or tries to act, on everything in direct contact with me." A faint smile. "Except Earth itself, if I happen to be barefoot. I suppose that much mass, bound together not only by gravitation but by other, even stronger forces, has a—what?—a cohesion?—of its own."

"You warned me against putting a solid object where you planned to, uh, materialize," I said.

"Right," he answered. "I can't, in that case. I've experimented. Traveling through time, I can move around meanwhile in space if I want. That's how I managed to appear next to myself. By the way, the surface I'm on may rise or sink, but I rise or sink likewise, same as when a person stands somewhere in normal time. And, aside from whatever walking I do, I stay on the same geographical spot. Never mind that this planet is spinning on its axis, and whirling around a sun which is rushing through a galaxy

. . . I stay *here*. Gravitation again, I suppose. . . . Yes, about solid matter. I tried entering a hill, when I was a child and thoughtless. I could go inside, all right, easy as stepping into a bank of fog. But then I was cut off from light, and I couldn't emerge into normal time, it was like being in concrete, and my breath ran out—" He shivered. "I barely made it back to the open air."

"I guess matter resists displacement by you," I ventured. "Fluids aren't too hard to shove aside when you emerge, but solids are."

"Uh-huh, that's what I figured. If I'd passed out and died inside that rock and dirt, I guess my body would've well, been carried along into the future at the ordinary rate, and fallen back into normal existence when at last the hill eroded away from around it."

"Amazing how you, a mere tad, kept the secret."

"Well, I gather I gave my mother a lot of worries. I don't actually remember. Who does recall his first few years? Probably I needed a while to realize I was unique, and the realization scared me—maybe time-traveling was a Bad Thing to do. Or perhaps I gloated. Anyway, Uncle Jack straightened me out."

"Was he the unknown who brought you back when you'd been lost?"

"Yes. I do remember that. I'd embarked on a long expedition into the past, looking for Indians. But I only found a forest. He showed up—having searched the area through a number of years—and we had it nice together. Finally he took my hand and showed me how to come home with him. He could've delivered me within a few minutes of my departure and spared my parents those dreadful hours. But I believe he wanted me to see how I'd hurt them, so the need for discretion would really get driven into me. It was."

His tone grew reminiscent: "We had some fine excursions later. Uncle Jack was the ideal guide and mentor. I'd no reason to disobey his commands about secrecy, aside from some disguised bragging to my friend Pete. Uncle Jack led me to better things than I'd ever have discovered for myself."

"You did hop around on your own," I reminded him.

"Occasionally. Like when a couple of bullies attacked me. I doubled back several times and outnumbered them."

"No wonder you showed such a growth rate. . . . When you learned your father was going into the service, you hoped to assure yourself he'd return safe, right?"

Jack Havig winced. "Yes. I headed futureward and took quick peeks at intervals. Until I looked in the window and saw Mother crying. Then I went pastward till I found a chance to read that telegram—oh, God. I didn't travel in time again for years. I didn't think I'd ever want to."

The silence of the snow lapped about us.

At length I asked: "When did you most recently meet this mentor?"

"In 1969. But the previous time had been . . . shortly before I took off and learned about my father. Uncle Jack was particularly good to me, then. We went to the old and truly kind of circus, sometime in the late nineteenth century. I wondered why he seemed so sad, and why he reexplained in such detail the necessity of keeping our secret. Now I know."

"Do you know who he is?"

His mouth lifted on the left side only. "Who do you suppose?"

"I resumed time traveling last year," he said after a while. "I had to have a refuge from that, that situation on the farm. They were jaunts into the past, at first. You've no idea how beautiful this country was before the settlers arrived. And the Indians—well, I have friends among them. I haven't acquired more than a few words of their language, but they welcome me and, uh, the girls are always ready, able, and eager."

I could not but laugh. "Sven the Younger makes a lot of your having no dates!"

He grinned back. "You can guess how those trips relieved me." Serious again: "But you can guess, too, how more and more the whole thing at home—what Birkelund is pleased to call my home—got to feel silly, futile, and stifling. Even the outside world. Like, what the devil was I doing in high school? There I was, full-grown, full of these marvels I'd seen, hearing teen-agers giggle and teachers drone!"

"I imagine the family flareup was what sent you into the future?"

"Right. I was half out of my mind with rage. Mainly I hoped to see Sven Birkelund's tombstone. Twenty years forward seemed like a good round number. But knowing I'd have a lot to catch up on, I made for late 1969, so as to be prepared to get the most out of 1970. . . . The house was still in existence. Is. Will be."

"Sven?" I asked softly.

"I suppose he'll have survived." His tone was savage. "I don't care enough to check on that. In two more years, my mother will divorce him."

"And—?"

"She'll take the babies, both of them, back to Massachusetts. Her third marriage will be good. I mustn't add to her worries in this time, though. That's why I returned. I made my absence a month long to show Birkelund I mean business; but I couldn't make it longer than that, I couldn't do it to her."

I saw in him what I have seen in others, when those they care about are sick or dying. So I was hasty to say: "You told me you met your Uncle Jack, your other self."

"Yeah." He was glad to continue with practicalities. "He was waiting when I appeared in 1969. That was out in the woodlot, at night—I didn't want to risk a stray spectator—but the lot had been logged off and planted in corn. He'd taken a double room at the hotel—that is, the one they'll build after the Senlac Arms is razed—and put me up for a few days. He told me about my mother, and encouraged me to verify it by newspaper files in the library, plus showing me a couple of letters she'd recently written to him . . . to me. Afterward he gave me a thousand dollars—Doc, the prices in twenty years!—and he suggested I look around the country.

"News magazines indicated Berkeley was where it was at—uh, a future idiom. Anyway, San Francisco's right across the Bay and I'd always wanted to see it."

"How was Berkeley?" I asked, remembering visits to a staid university town.

He told me, as well as he was able. But no words, in 1951, could have conveyed what I have since experienced, that wild, eerie, hilarious, terrifying, grotesque, mind-bending assault upon every sense and common sense which is Telegraph Avenue at the close of the seventh decade of the twentieth century.

"Didn't you risk trouble with the police?" I inquired.

"No. I stopped off in 1966 and registered under a fake name for the draft, which gave me a card saying I was twenty-one in 1969. . . . The street people hooked me. I came to them, an old-fashioned bumpkin, heard their version of what'd been going on, and nobody else's. For months I was among the radicals. Hand-to-mouth odd-job existence, demonstrations, pot, dirty pad, unbathed girls, the works."

"Your writing here doesn't seem favorable to that," I observed.

"No. I'm sure Uncle Jack wanted me to have an inside

knowledge, how it feels to be somebody who's foresworn the civilization that bred him. But I changed."

"M-m-m, I'd say you rebounded. Way out into right field. But go on. What happened?"

"I took a trip to the further future."

"And?"

"Doc," he said most quietly, "consider yourself fortunate. You're already getting old."

"I'll be dead, then?" My heart stumbled.

"By the time of the blowup and breakdown, no doubt. I haven't checked, except I did establish you're alive and healthy in 1970." I wondered why he did not smile, as he should have done when giving me good news. Today I know; he said nothing about Kate.

"The war—*the* war—and its consequences come later," he went on in the same iron voice. "But everything follows straight from that witches' sabbath I saw part of in Berkeley."

He sighed and rubbed his tired eyes. "I returned to 1970 with some notion of stemming the tide. There were a few people around, even young people, who could see a little reality. This broadside . . . they helped me publish and distribute it, thinking me a stray Republican."

"Were you?"

"Lord, no. You don't imagine any political party has been any use whatsoever for the past three or four generations, do you? They'll get worse."

He had emptied his glass anew, but declined my offer of more. "I'd better keep a clear head, Doc. We do have to work out a cover yarn. I know we will, because my not-so-much-older self gave me to understand I'd handle my present troubles all right. However, it doesn't let us off going through the motions."

"Time is unchangeable?" I wondered. "We—our lives—

are caught and held in the continuum—like flies in amber?"

"I don't know, I don't know," he groaned. "I do know that my efforts were wasted. My former associates called me a fink, my new friends were an insignificant minority, and, hell, we could hardly give away our literature."

"You mustn't expect miracles in politics," I said. "Beware of the man who promises them."

"True. I realized as much, after the shock of what I'd seen uptime had faded a bit. In fact, I decided my duty was to come back and stand by my mother. At least this way I can make the world a tiny bit less horrible."

His tone softened: "No doubt I was foolish to keep a copy of my flyer. But the dearest girl helped me put it together. . . . Well. In a way, I've lucked out. Now one other human being shares my life. I've barely started to feel how lonely I was."

"You are absolutely unique?" I whispered.

"I don't know. I'd guess not. They're doubtless very rare, but surely more time travelers than me exist. How can I find them?" he cried. "And if we should join together, what can we do?"

chapter 5

Birkelund proved less of a problem than expected. I saw him in private, told him the writing was a leftover script from an amateur show, and pointed out that it was actually sarcastic—after which I gave him holy hell about his treatment of his stepson and his wife. He took it with ill grace, but he took it. As remarked earlier, he was by no means an evil man.

Still, the situation remained explosive. Jack contributed, being daily more short-tempered and self-willed. "He's changed so much," Eleanor told me in grief. "His very appearance. And I can't blame all the friction on Sven and his boys. Jack's often downright arrogant."

Of course he was, in his resentment of home, his boredom in school, his burden of foreknowledge. But I couldn't tell his mother that. Nor, for her sake, could he make more than overnight escapes for the next two or three years.

"I think," I said, "it'd be best if he took off on his own."

"Bob, he's barely eighteen," she protested.

He was at least twenty-one, probably more, I knew.

"Old enough to join the service." He'd registered in the lawful manner on his birthday. "That'll give him a chance to find himself. It's possible to be drafted by request, so as to be in for the minimum period. The board will oblige if I speak to 'em."

"Not before he's graduated!"

I understood her dismay and disappointment. "He can take correspondence courses, Ellie. Or the services offer classes, which a bright lad like Jack can surely get into. I'm afraid this is our best bet."

He had already agreed to the idea. A quick uptime hop showed him he would be posted to Europe. "I can explore a lot of history," he said; then, chill: "Besides, I'd better learn about weapons and combat techniques. I damn near got killed in the twenty-first century. Couple members of a cannibal band took me by surprise, and if I hadn't managed to wrench free for an instant—"

The Army was ill-suited to his temperament, but he stuck out basic training, proceeded into electronics, and on the whole gained by the occasion. To be sure, much of that was due to his excursions downtime. They totaled a pair of extra years.

His letters to me could only hint at this, since Kate would read them too. It was a hard thing for me, not to open for her the tremendous fact, not to have her beside me when at last he came home and through hour upon hour showed me his notes, photographs, memories.

(Details were apt to be unglamorous—problems of vaccination, language, transportation, money, law, custom—filth, vermin, disease, cruelty, tyranny, violence—"Doc, I'd never dreamed how different medieval man was. Huge variations from place to place and era to era, yeah, but always the . . . Orientalness? . . . no, probably it's just that the Orient has changed less." However, he had watched Caesar's legions in triumph through Rome, and the greyhound shapes of Viking craft dancing over Oslo Fjord, and Leonardo da Vinci at work. . . . He'd not been able to observe in depth. In fact, he was maddened by the superficial quality of almost all his experiences. How much can you learn in a totally strange environment, when you can barely speak a word and are liable to be arrested on suspicion before you can swap for a suit of contemporary clothes? Yet what would I not have given to be there too?)

How it felt like betrayal of Kate, not telling her! But if Jack could keep silence toward his mother, I must toward my wife. His older *persona* had been, was, would be right in stamping upon the child a reflex of secrecy.

Consider the consequences, had it become known that one man—or one little boy—can swim through time. To be the sensation of the age is no fit fate for any human. In this case, imagine as well the demands, appeals, frantic attempts by the greedy, the power-hungry, the ideology-besotted, the bereaved, the frightened to use him, the race between governments to sequester or destroy him who could be the ultimate spy or unstoppable assassin. If he survived, and his sanity did, he would soon have no choice but to flee into another era and there keep his talent hidden.

No, best wear a mask from the beginning.

But then what use was the fantastic gift?

"Toward the end of my hitch, I spent more time thinking than roving," he said.

We'd taken my boat out on Lake Winnego. He'd come home, discharged, a few weeks earlier, but much remained to tell me. This was the more true because his mother needed his moral support in her divorce from Birkelund, her move away from scenes which were now painful. He'd matured further, not only in the flesh. Two of my years ago, a man had confronted me: but a very young man, still groping his way out of hurt and bewilderment. The Jack Havig who sat in the cockpit today was in full command of himself.

I shifted my pipe and put down the helm. We came about in a heel and *swoosh* and rattle of boom. Springtime glittered on blue water; sweetness breathed from the green across fields and trees, from apple blossoms and fresh-turned earth. The wind whooped. It was cool and a hawk rode upon it.

"Well, you had plenty to think about," I answered.

"For openers," he said, "how does time travel work?"

"Tell me, Mr. Bones, how *does* time travel work?"

He did not chuckle. "I learned a fair amount of basic physics in the course of becoming an electronics technician. And I read a lot on my own, including stuff I went uptime to consult—books, future issues of *Scientific American* and *Nature*, et cetera. All theory says that what I do is totally impossible. It starts by violating the conservation of energy and goes on from there."

"E pur si muove."

"Huh? . . . Oh. Yeah. Doc, I studied the Italian Renaissance prior to visiting it, and discovered Galileo never did say that. Nor did he ever actually drop weights off the Leaning Tower of Pisa. Well." He sprawled back on the bench and opened another bottle of beer for each of us. "Okay. So there are hookers in the conservation of energy that official science doesn't suspect. Mathematically speaking, world lines are allowed to have finite, if not infinite discontinuities, and to be multi-valued functions. In many ways, time travel is equivalent to faster-than-light travel, which the physicists also declare is impossible."

I watched my tobacco smoke stream off on the breeze, Wavelets smacked. "You've left me a few light-years behind," I said. "I get nothing out of your lecture except an impression that you don't believe anything, uh, supernatural is involved."

He nodded. "Right. Whatever the process may be, it operates within natural law. It's essentially physical. Matter-energy relationships are involved. Well, then, why can I do it, and nobody else? I've been forced to conclude it's a peculiarity in my genes."

"Oh?"

"They'll find the molecular basis of heredity, approximately ten years from now."

"What?" I sat bolt upright. "This you've got to tell me more about!"

"Later, later. I'll give you as much information on DNA and the rest as I can, though that isn't a whale of a lot. The point is, our genes are not simply a blueprint for building a fetus. They operate throughout life, by controlling enzyme production. You might well call them the very stuff of life. . . . What besides enzymes can be involved? This civilization is going to destroy itself before they've answered that question. But I suspect there's some kind of resonance—or something—in those enormous molecules: and if your gene structure chances to resonate precisely right, you're a time traveler."

"Well, an interesting hypothesis." I had fallen into a habit of understatement in his presence.

"I've empirical evidence," he replied. With an effort: "Doc, I've had quite a few women. Not in this decade; I'm too stiff and gauche. But uptime and downtime, periods when it's fairly easy and I can use a certain glamour of mysteriousness."

"Congratulations," I said for lack of anything better.

He squinted across the lake. "I'm not callous about them," he said. "I mean, well, if a romp is all she wants, like those Dakotan girls two-three centuries ago, okay, fine. But if the affair is anything more, I feel responsible. I may not plan to live out my life in her company—I wonder if I'll ever marry—but I check on her future for the next several years, and try to make sure she does well." His countenance twisted a bit. "Or as well as a mortal can. I've not got the moral courage to search out their deaths."

After a pause: "I'm digressing, but it's an important digression to me. Take Meg, for instance, I was in Elizabethan London. The problems caused by my ignorance were less than in most milieus, though I did need a while to learn the ropes and even the pronunciation of their English. A silver ingot I'd brought along converted more easily than usual to coin—people today don't realize how much suspicion and regulation there was in the oh-so-swashbuckling past—even if I do think the dealer cheated me. Well, anyhow, I could lodge in a lovely half-timbered inn, and go to the Globe, and generally have a ball.

"One day I happened to be in a slum district. A woman plucked my sleeve and offered me her daughter's maidenhead cheap. I was appalled, but thought I should at least meet the poor girl, maybe give her money, maybe try to get my landlord to take her on as a respectable servant. . . . No way." (Another of his anachronistic turns of speech.) "She was nervous and determined. And after she'd explained, I had to agree that an alley lass of independent spirit probably was better off as a whore than a servant, considering what servants had to put up with. Not that anyone was likely to take her in such a capacity, class distinctions and antagonisms being what they were.

"She was cocky, she was good-looking, she said she'd rather it was me than some nasty and probably poxy dotard. What could I do? Disinterested benevolence just plain was not in her mental universe. If she couldn't see my selfish motive, she'd've decided it must be too deep and horrible for her, and fled."

He glugged his beer. "All right," he told me defiantly.

"I moved into larger quarters and took her along. The idea of an age of consent didn't exist either. Forget about our high school kids; I'd certainly never touch one of them. Meg was a woman, young but a woman. We lived together for four years of her life.

"Of course, for me that was a matter of paying the rent in advance, and now and then coming back from the twentieth century. Not very often, I being stationed in France. Sure, I could leave whenever I wanted, and return with no AWOL time passed, but the trip to England cost, and besides, there were all those other centuries. . . . Nevertheless, I do believe Meg was faithful. You should've seen how she fended off her relatives who thought they could batten on me! I told her I was in the Dutch diplomatic service. . . .

"Oh, skip the details. I'm talking all around my subject. In the end, a decent young journeyman fell in love with her. I gave them a wedding present and my blessings. And I checked ahead, dropping in occasionally through the next decade, to make sure everything was all right. It was, as close as could be expected."

He sighed. "To get to the point, Doc, she bore him half a dozen children, starting inside a year of their marriage. She had never conceived by me. As far as I've determined, no woman ever has."

He had gotten a fertility test, according to which he was normal.

Neither of us wanted to dwell on his personal confession. It suggested too strongly how shaped our psyches are by whatever happens to be around us. "You mean," I said slowly, "you're a mutant? So much a mutant that you count as, as a different species?"

"Yeah. I think my genes are that strange."

"But a fellow time traveler—a female—"

"Right on, Doc." Another futurism.

He was still for a while, in the blowing sunlit day, before he said: "Not that that's important in itself. What is important—maybe the most important thing in Earth's whole existence—is to find those other travelers, if there are any, and see what we can do about the horrors uptime. I can't believe I'm a meaningless accident!"

"How do you propose to go about it?"

His gaze was cat-cool. "I start by becoming rich."

For years which followed, I am barely on the edge of his story.

He'd see me at intervals, I think more to keep our friendship alive than to bring me up to date—since he obviously wanted Kate's company as much as mine. But I have only indirect news of his career. Often, in absence, he would become a dream in my mind, so foreign was he to our day-by-day faster-and-faster-aging small-town life, the growing up of our sons, the adventure of daughters-in-law and grandchildren. But then he would return, as if out of night, and for hours I would again be dominated by that lonely, driven man.

I don't mean he was fanatical. In fact, he continued to gain in perspective and in the skill of savoring this world. His intellect ranged widely, though it's clear that history and anthropology must be his chief concerns. As a drop of fortune, he had a talent for learning languages. (He and I wondered how many time travelers were wing-clipped by the mere lack of that.) Sardonic humor and traditional Midwestern courtesy combined to make his presence pleasant. He became quite a gourmet, while staying able to live on stockfish and hardtack without complaint. He kept a schooner in Boston, whereon he took Kate and me to the West Indies in celebration of our retirement. While the usages of his boyhood made him reticent about it, I learned he was deeply sensitive to beauty both natural and man-made; of the latter, he had a special fondness for baroque, classical, and Chinese music, for fine ships and weapons, and for Hellenic architecture. (God, if You exist, I do thank You from my inmost heart that I have seen Jack Havig's photographs of the unruined Acropolis.)

I was the single sharer of his secret, but not his single friend. Theoretically he could have been intimate with everyone great, Moses, Pericles, Shakespeare, Lincoln, Einstein. But in practice the obstacles were too much. Besides language, custom, and law, the famous were hedged off by being busy, conspicuous, sought-after. No, Havig—I called him "Jack" to his face, but now it seems more natural to write his surname—Havig told me about people like his lively little Meg (three hundred years dust), or a mountain man who accompanied Lewis and Clark, or a profane old *moustache* who had marched with Napoleon.

("History does not tend to the better, Doc, it does not, it does not. We imagine so because events have produced our glorious selves. Think, however. Put aside the romantic legends and look at the facts. The average Frenchman in 1800 was no more unfree than the average Englishman. The French Empire could have brought Europe together, and could have been liberalized from within, and there might have been no World War I in which Western civilization cut its own throat. Because that's what happened, you know. We're still busy bleeding to death, but we haven't far to go now.")

Mainly his time excursions were for fun, in that period between his acquiring the techniques and resources to make them effective, and his development of a search plan for fellow mutants. "To be honest," he grinned, "I find myself more and more fond of low-down life."

"Toulouse-Lautrec's Paris?" I asked at random. He had already told me that earlier decadences were overrated, or at least consisted of tight-knit upper classes which didn't welcome strangers.

"Well, I haven't tried there," he admitted. "An idea, maybe. On the other hand, Storyville in its flowering—" He wasn't interested in the prostitutes; if nothing else, he had by now seen enough of the human condition to know how gruesome theirs usually was. He went for the jazz, and for the company of people whom he said were more real than most of his own generation, not to speak of 1970.

Meanwhile he made his fortune.

You suppose that was easy. Let him look up the stock market quotations—1929 is an obvious year—and go surf on the tides of Wall Street.

The fact was different. For instance, what might he use for money?

While in Europe, he bought gold or silver out of his pay, which he exchanged for cash in various parts of the nineteenth and later eighteenth centuries. With that small stake, he could begin trading. He would take certain stamps and coins uptime and sell them to dealers; he would go downtime with a few aluminum vessels, which were worth more than gold before the Hall process was invented. But these and similar dealings were necessarily on a minute scale, both because the mass he could carry was limited and because he dared not draw overmuch attention to himself.

He considered investing and growing wealthy in that period, but rejected the idea. The rules and mores were too peculiar, too intricate for him to master in as much of his lifespan as he cared to spend. Besides, he wanted to be based in his own original era; if nothing else, he would need swift spatial transportation when he began his search. Thus he couldn't simply leave money in the semi-distant past at compound interest. The intervening years gave too many chances for something to go wrong.

As for a more manageable point like 1929, what gold he brought would represent a comparatively trifling sum. Shuttling back and forth across those frantic days, he could parlay it—but within strict limits, if he wasn't to be unduly noticed. Also, he must take assorted federal agencies into account, which in the years ahead would become ever better equipped to be nosy.

He never gave me the details of his operations. "Frankly," he said, "finance bores me like an auger. I found me a couple of sharp partners who'd front, and an ultra-solid bank for a trustee, and let them make more off my 'economic analyses' than was strictly necessary."

In effect, John Franklin Havig established a fund, including an arrangement for taxes and the like, which was to be paid over to "any collateral male descendant" who met certain unambiguous standards, upon the twenty-first birthday of this person. As related, the bank was one of those eastern ones, with Roman pillars and cathedral dimness and, I suspect, a piece of Plymouth Rock in a reliquary. Thus when John Franklin Havig, collateral descendant, was contacted in 1964, everything was so discreet that he entered his millionaire condition with scarcely a ripple. The Senlac *Trumpet* did announce that he had received a substantial inheritance from a distant relative.

"I let the bank keep on managing the bucks," he told me. "What I do is write checks."

After all, riches were merely his means to an end.

No, several ends. I've mentioned his pleasures. I should add the help he gave his mother and, quietly, others. On the whole, he disdained recognized charities. "They're big businesses," he said. "Their executives draw down more money than you do, Doc. Besides, to be swinishly blunt, we have too many people. When you've seen the Black

Death, you can't get excited about Mississippi sharecroppers." I scolded him amicably for being such a right-winger when he had witnessed *laissez-faire* in action, and he retorted amicably that in this day and age liberals like me were the ones who had learned nothing and forgotten nothing, and we had us a drink. . . . But I believe that, without fuss, he rescued quite a few individuals; and it is a fact that he was a substantial contributor to the better conservationist organizations.

"We need a reserve of life, every kind of life," he explained. "Today for the spirit—a glimpse of space and green. Tomorrow for survival, flat-out survival."

The War of Judgment, he said, would by no means be the simple capitalist-versus-Communist slugfest which most of us imagined in the 1950's.

"I've only the vaguest idea yet of what actually will go on. Not surprising. I've had to make fugitive appearances—watching out for radioactivity and a lot else—and who in the immediate sequel is in any condition to give me a reasoned analysis? Hell, Doc, scholars argue today about what went wrong in 1914 to '18, and they aren't scrambling for a leftover can of dogfood, or arming against the Mong who'll pour across a Bering Straits that all the dust kicked into the atmosphere will cause to be frozen."

His impression was that, like World War I, it was a conflict which everybody anticipated, nobody wanted, and men would have recoiled from had they foreseen the consequences. He thought it was less ideological than ecological.

"I have this nightmare notion that it came not just as a result of huge areas turning into deserts, but came barely in time. Do you know the oceans supply half our oxygen? By 1970, insecticide was in the plankton. By 1990, every ocean was scummy, and stank, and you didn't dare swim in it."

"But this must have been predicted," I said.

He leered. "Yeah. 'Environment' was very big for a while. Ecology Now stickers on the windshields of cars belonging to hairy young men—cars which dripped oil wherever they parked and took off in clouds of smoke thicker than your pipe can produce. . . . Before long, the fashionable cause was something else, I forget what. Anyhow, that whole phase—the wave after wave of causes—passed away. People completely stopped caring.

"You see, that was the logical conclusion of the whole trend. I know it's stupid to assign a single blame for something as vast as the War of Judgment, its forerunners and aftermaths. Especially when I'm still in dark about what the events *were*. But Doc, I feel a moral certainty that a large part of the disaster grew from this particular country, the world's most powerful, the vanguard country for things both good and ill . . . never really trying to meet the responsibilities of power.

"We'll make halfhearted attempts to stop some enemies in Asia, and because the attempts are halfhearted we'll piss away human lives—on both sides—and treasure—to no purpose. Hoping to placate the implacable, we'll estrange our last few friends. Men elected to national office will solemnly identify inflation with rising prices, which is like identifying red spots with the measles virus, and slap on wage and price controls, which is like papering the cracks in a house whose foundations are sliding away. So economic collapse brings international impotence. The well-off whites will grow enough aware that we have distressed minorities, and give them enough, to bring on revolt without really helping them; and the revolt will bring on reaction, which will stamp on every remnant of progress. As for our foolish little attempts to balance what we drain from the environment against what we put back—well, I mentioned that car carrying the ecology sticker.

"At first Americans will go on any orgy of guilt. Later they'll feel inadequate. Finally they'll turn apathetic. After all, they'll be able to buy any anodyne, any pseudo-existence they want.

"I wonder if at the end, down underneath, they don't welcome their own multimillionfold deaths."

Thus in February of 1964, Havig came into the inheritance he had made for himself. Shortly thereafter he set about shoring up his private past, and spent months of his lifespan being "Uncle Jack." I asked him what the hurry was, and he said, "Among other things, I want to get as much foreknowledge as possible behind me." I considered that for a while, and choked off my last impulse to ask him about the tomorrows of me and mine. I did not understand how rich a harvest this would bear until the day when they buried Kate.

I never asked Havig if he had seen her gravestone earlier. He may have, and kept silent. As a physician, I think I know how it is possible to possess such information and yet smile.

He didn't go straight from one episode with his childhood self to the next. That would have been monotonous. Instead, he made his pastward visits vacations from his studies at our state university. He didn't intend to be frustrated when again he sought a non-English-speaking milieu. Furthermore, he needed a baseline from which to extrapolate changes of language in the future; there/then he was also often a virtual deaf-mute.

His concentration was on Latin and Greek—the latter that *koinê* which in its various forms had wider currency through both space and time than Classical Attic—plus French, German, Italian, Spanish, Portugese (and English), with emphasis on their evolution—plus some Hebrew, Aramaic, Arabic—plus quite a bit of the numerous Polynesian tongues.

"They do have a civilization on the other side of the dark centuries," he told me. "I've barely glimpsed that, and can't make head or tail of what's going on. But it does look as if Pacific Ocean peoples dominate the world, speaking the damnedest *lingua franca* you can imagine."

"So there is hope!" gusted from me.

"I still have to find out for sure." His glance speared mine. "Look, suppose you were a time traveler from, well, Egypt of the Pharaohs. Suppose you came to today's world and touristed around, trying to stay anonymous. How much sense would anything make? Would the question 'Is this development good or bad?' even be meaningful to you? I haven't tried to explore beyond the early stages of the Maurai Federation. It'll be the work of years to understand that much."

He was actually more interested in bygone eras, which to him were every bit as alive as today or tomorrow. Those he could study beforehand—in more detail than you might think, unless you're a professional historiographer—and thus prepare himself to move around with considerable freedom. Besides, while the past had ghastlinesses enough, nothing, not the Black Death or the burning of heretics or the Middle Passage or the Albigensian Crusade, nothing in his mind matched the Judgment. "That's when the whole planet almost goes under," he said. "I imagine my fellow time travelers generally avoid it. I'm likeliest to find them in happier, or less unhappy, eras."

Given these activities, he was biologically about thirty when at last he succeeded. This was in Jerusalem, on the day of the Crucifixion.

chapter 6

He told me of his plan in 1964. As far as practicable, his policy was to skip intervals of the twentieth century equal to those he spent elsewhere, so that his real and calendar ages wouldn't get too much out of step. I hadn't seen him for a while. He no longer dwelt in Senlac, but made his headquarters in New York—a post-office box in the present, a sumptuous apartment in the 1890's, financed by the sale of gold he bought after this was again made legal and carried downtime. He did come back for visits, though. Kate found that touching. I did too, but I knew besides what need he had of me, his only confidant.

"Why . . . you're right!" I exclaimed. "The moment you'd expect every traveler, at least in Christendom, to head for. Why haven't you done it before?"

"Less simple than you suppose, Doc," he replied. "That's a long haul, to a most thoroughly alien territory. And how certain is the date, anyway? Or even the fact?"

I blinked. "You mean you've never considered seeking the historical Christ? I know you're not religious, but surely the mystery around him—"

"Doc, what he was, or if he was, makes only an academic difference. What counts is what people through the ages have believed. My life expectancy isn't enough for me to do the pure research I'd like. In fact, I'm overdue to put fun and games aside. I've seen too much human misery. Time travel has got to have some real value; it's got to be made to help." He barely smiled. "You know I'm no saint. But I do have to live in my own head."

He flew from New York to Israel in 1969, while the Jews were in firm control of Jerusalem and a visitor could move around freely. From his hotel he walked out Jericho Road, carrying a handbag, till he found an orange grove which offered concealment. There he sprang back to the previous midnight and made his preparations.

The Arab costume he had bought at a tourist shop would pass in Biblical times. A knife, more eating tool than weapon, was sheathed at his hip; being able to blink out of bad situations, he seldom took a firearm. A leather purse held phrase book (specially compiled, for pay, by an American graduate student), food, drinking cup, Halazone tablets, soap, flea repellent, antibiotic, and money. That last was several coins of the Roman period, plus a small ingot he could exchange if need be.

Having stowed his modern clothes in the bag, he drew forth his last item of equipment. He called it a chronolog. It was designed and built to his specifications in 1980, to take advantage of the superb solid-state electronics then available. The engineers who made it had perhaps required less ingenuity than Havig had put into his cover story.

I have seen the apparatus. It's contained in a green crackle-finish box with a carrying handle, about 24 by 12 by 6 inches. When the lid is opened, you can fold out an optical instrument vaguely suggestive of a sextant, and you can set the controls and read the meters. Beneath these lies a miniature but most sophisticated computer, running off a nickel-cadmium battery. The weight is about five pounds, which edges near half the limit of what a traveler can pack through time and helps explain Havig's reluctance to carry a gun. Other items are generally more useful. But none approaches in value the chronolog.

Imagine. He projects himself backward or forward to a chosen moment. How does he know "when" he has arrived? On a short hop, he can count days, estimate the hour by sun or stars if a clock isn't on the spot. But a thousand years hold a third of a million dawns; and the chances are that many of them won't be identifiable, because of stormy weather or the temporary existence of a building or some similar accident.

Havig took his readings. The night was clear, sufficiently cold for his breath to smoke; Jerusalem's lights hazed the sky northward, but elsewhere the country lay still and dark save for outlying houses and passing cars; constellations wheeled brilliant overhead. He placed the moon and two planets in relation to them, set the precise Greenwich time and geographical locations on appropriate dim-glowing dials, and worked a pair of verniers till he had numbers corresponding to that Passover week of Anno Domini 33.

("The date does seem well established," he'd remarked. "At least, it's the one everybody would aim at." He laughed. "Beats the Nativity. The only thing certain about *that* is it wasn't at midwinter—not if shepherds were away from home watching their flocks!")

He had been breathing in and out, deep slow breaths which oxygenated his blood to the fullest. Now he took a lungful—not straining, which would have spent energy, just storing a fair amount—and launched himself down the world lines.

There was the sensation, indescribable, but which he had told me was not quite unlike swimming against a high tide. The sun rose in the west and skidded eastward; then, as he "accelerated," light became a vague pulsation of grayness, and everywhere around him reached shadow. It was altogether silent.

He glimpsed a shellburst—soundless, misty—but was at once past the Six Day War, or had that been the War of Independence or the First World War? Wan unshapes drifted past. On a cloudy night in the late nineteenth century he must reenter normal time for air. The chronolog could have given him the exact date, had he wanted to shoot the stars again; its detectors included sensitivities to those radiations which pierce an overcast. But no point in that. A couple of mounted men, probably Turkish soldiers, happened to be near. Their presence had been too brief for him to detect while traveling, even were it daylight. They didn't notice him in the dark. Horseshoes thumped by and away.

He continued.

Dim though it was, the landscape began noticeably changing. Contours remained about the same, but now there were many trees, now few, now there was desert, now planted fields. Fleetingly, he glimpsed what he guessed was a great wooden stadium wherein the Crusaders held tourneys before Saladin threw them out of their bloodsmeared kingdom, and he was tempted to pause but held to his purpose. Stops for breath grew more frequent as he neared his goal. The journey drained strength; and, too, the idea that he might within hours achieve his dream made the heart hammer in his breast.

A warning light blinked upon the chronolog.

It could follow sun, moon, planets, and stars with a speed and precision denied to flesh. It could allow for precession, perturbation, proper motion, even continental drift; and when it identified an aspect of heaven corresponding to the destination, that could be nothing except the hour which was sought.

A light flashed red, and Havig stopped.

* * *

Thursday night was ending. If the Bible spoke truly, the Last Supper had been held, the agony in the garden was past, and Jesus lay in bonds, soon to be brought before Pilate, condemned, scourged, lashed to the cross, pierced, pronounced dead, and laid in the tomb.

("They tie them in place," Havig told me. "Nails wouldn't support the weight; the hands would tear apart. Sometimes nails are driven in for special revenge, so the tradition could be right as far as it goes." He covered his face. "Doc, I've seen them hanging, tongues black from thirst, bellies bloated—after a while they don't cry out any longer, they croak, and no mind is left behind their eyes. The stink, the stink! They often take days to die. I wonder if Jesus wasn't physically frail, he won to his death so soon. . . . A few friends and kinfolk, maybe, hover on the fringes of the crowd, hardly ever daring to speak or even weep. The rest crack jokes, gamble, drink, eat picnic lunches, hold the kiddies up for a better view. What kind of a thing is man, anyway?"

(Put down your pride. Ours is the century of Buchenwald and Vorkuta—and Havig reminded me of what had gone on in the nostalgically remembered Edwardian part of it, in places like the Belgian Congo and the southern United States—and he told me of what has yet to happen. Maybe I don't envy him his time travel after all.)

Morning made an eastward whiteness. Now he had an olive orchard at his back, beyond which he glimpsed a huddle of adobe buildings. The road was a rutted dirt track. Afar, half hidden in lingering twilight, Jerusalem of the Herodian kings and the Roman proconsulate crouched on its hills. It was smaller and more compact than the city he remembered two millennia hence, mainly within walls though homesteads did spread beyond. Booths and felt tents crowded near the gates, erected by provincials come to the holy place for the holy days. The air was cold and smelled of earth. Birds twittered. "Beyond one or two hundred years back," Havig once said to me, "the daytime sky is always full of wings."

He sat panting while light quickened and vigor returned. Hungry, he broke off chunks of goat cheese and tortilla-like bread, and was surprised to realize that he was taking a perfectly ordinary meal on the first Good Friday in the world.

If it was. The scholars might have gotten the date wrong, or Jesus might be nothing more than an Osirian-Essene-Mithraic myth. Suppose he wasn't, though? Suppose he was, well, maybe not the literal incarnation of the Creator of these acres, those wildfowl, yonder universe . . . but at least the prophet from whose vision stemmed most of what was decent in all time to come. Could a life be better spent than following him on his ministry?

Well, Havig would have to become fluent in Aramaic, plus a million details of living, and he would have to forget his quest. . . . He sighed and rose. The sun broke over the land.

He soon had company. Nevertheless he walked as an outsider.

("If anything does change man," he said, "it's science and technology. Just think about the fact—while it lasts—that parents need not take for granted some of their babies will die. You get a completely different concept of what a child is." He must have seen the memory of Nora flit across my face, for he laid a hand on my shoulder and said: "I'm sorry, Doc. Shouldn't have mentioned that. And never ask me to take a camera back to her, or a shot of penicillin, because I've tried altering the known past and something always happens to stop me. . . . Think of electric bulbs, or even candles. When the best you've got is a flickering wick in a bowl of oil, you're pretty well tied to daylight. The simple freedom to stay awake late isn't really that simple. It has all sorts of subtle but far-reaching effects on the psyche.")

Folk were up at dawn, tending livestock, hoeing weeds, stoking fires, cooking and cleaning, against the Sabbath tomorrow. Bearded men in ragged gowns whipped starveling donkeys, overloaded with merchandise, toward the city. Children, hardly begun to walk, scattered grain for poultry; a little older, they shooed gaunt stray dogs from the lambs. When he reached pavement, Havig was jostled: by caravaneers from afar, sheikhs, priests, hideous beggars, farmers, artisans, a belated and very drunken harlot, a couple of Anatolian traders, or whatever they were, in cylindrical hats, accompanying a man in a Grecian tunic, and then the harsh cry to make way and tramp-tramp-tramp, quickstep and metal, a Roman squad returning from night patrol.

I've seen photographs which he took on different occasions, and can well imagine this scene. It was less gaudy than you may suppose, who live in an age of aniline dyes and fluorescents. Fabrics were subdued brown, gray, blue, cinnabar, and dusty. But the sound was enormous—shrill voices, laughter, oaths, extravagant lies and boasts, plang of a harp, fragments of a song; shuffling feet, clopping unshod hoofs, creaking wooden wheels, yelping dogs, bleating sheep, grunting camels, always and always the birds of springtime. These people were not stiff Englishmen or Americans; no, they windmilled their arms, they shaped the air with their palms, backslapped, jigged, clapped hand to dagger in affront and almost instantly were good-humored again. And the smells! The sweet sweat of horses, the sour sweat of men; smoke, fragrant from cedar or pungent from dried dung; new-baked bread; leeks and garlic and rancid grease; everywhere the droppings and passings of animals, often the ammonia of a compost heap; a breath of musk and attar of roses, as a veiled woman went by borne in a litter; a wagonload of fresh lumber; saddle leather warming beneath the sun—Havig never praised this day when nails were beaten through living bodies; but nothing of what he inhaled made him choke, or hurt his eyes, or gave him emphysema or cancer.

The gates of Jerusalem stood open. His pulse beat high.

And then he was found.

It happened all at once. Fingers touched his back. He turned and saw a stocky, wide-faced person, not tall, clad similarly to him but also beardless, short-haired, and fair-skinned.

Perspiration sheened upon the stranger's countenance. He braced himself against the streaming and shoving of the crowd and said through its racket: *"Es tu peregrinator temporis?"*

The accent was thick—eighteenth-century Polish, it would turn out—but Havig had a considerable mastery of classical as well as later Latin, and understood.

"Are you a time traveler?"

For a moment he could not reply. Reality whirled about him. Here was the end of his search.

Or theirs.

His height was unusual in this place, and he had left his head bare to show the barbering and the Nordic features. Unlike the majority of communities in history, Herodian Jerusalem was sufficiently cosmopolitan to let foreigners in; but his hope had been that others like him would guess he was a stranger in time as well as in space, or he might spy one of them. And now his hope was fulfilled.

His first thought, before the joy began, was an uneasy idea that this man looked far too tough.

* * *

They sat in a tavern which was their rendezvous and talked: Waclaw Krasicki who left Warsaw in 1738, Juan Mendoza who left Tijuana in 1924, and the pilgrims they had found.

These were Jack Havig. And Coenraad van Leuven, a man-at-arms from thirteenth-century Brabant, who had drawn his sword and tried to rescue the Savior as the cross was being carried toward Golgotha, and was urged back by Krasicki one second before a Roman blade would have spilled his guts, and now sat stunned by the question: "How do you know that person really was your Lord?" And a gray-bearded Orthodox monk who spoke only Croatian (?) but seemed to be named Boris and from the seventeenth century. And a thin, stringy-haired, pock-marked woman who hunched glaze-eyed in her robe and cowl and muttered in a language that nobody could identify.

"This is *all*?" Havig asked unbelievingly.

"Well, we have several more agents in town," Krasicki answered. Their conversation was in English, when the American's origin was known. "We're to meet Monday evening, and then again right after, hm, Pentecost. I suppose they'll turn up a few more travelers. But on the whole, yes, it seems like we'll make less of a haul than we expected."

Havig looked around. The shop was open-fronted. Customers sat crosslegged on shabby rugs, the street and its traffic before them, while they drank out of clay cups which a boy filled from a wineskin. Jerusalem clamored past. On Good Friday!

Krasicki wasn't bothered. He had mentioned leaving his backward city, country, and time for the French Enlightenment; in a whisper, he had labeled his partner Mendoza as a gangster. ("Mercenary" was what he said, but the connotation was plain.) "It's nothing to me if a Jewish carpenter who suffers from delirium is executed," he told Havig.

With a nudge: "Nor to you, eh? We seem to have gotten one reasonable recruit, at any rate."

In fact, that was not the American's attitude. He avoided argument by asking: "Are time travelers really so few?"

Krasicki shrugged. "Who knows? At least they can't easily come here. It makes sense. You boarded a flying machine and arrived in hours. But think of the difficulties, the downright impossibility of the trip, in most eras. We read about medieval pilgrims. But how many were they, really, in proportion to population? How many died on the way? Also, I suppose, we'll fail to find some time travelers because they don't want to be found—or, maybe, it's never occurred to them that others of their kind are in search—and their disguises will be too good for us."

Havig stared at him, and at imperturbable Juan Mendoza, three-quarters drunk Coenraad, filthy rosary-clicking Boris, unknown crazy woman, and thought: *Sure. Why should the gift fall exclusively on my type? Why didn't I expect it's given at random, to a complete cross-section of humanity? And I've seen what most humanity is like. And what makes me imagine I'm anything special?*

"We can't spend too much man-hours hunting, either," Krasicki said. "We are so few in the Eyrie." He patted Havig's knee. "Mother of God, how glad the Sachem will be that at least we found you!"

A third-century Syrian hermit and a second-century B.C. Ionian adventurer were gathered by two more teams. Report was given of another woman—she seemed to be a Coptic Christian—who vanished when approached.

"A rotten harvest," Krasicki grumbled. "However—" And he led the way, first to the stop after Pentecost, which yielded naught, then to the twenty-first century.

Dust drifted across desert. In Jerusalem nothing human remained except bones and shaped stones. But an aircraft waited, needle-nosed, stubby-winged, nuclear-powered, taken by Eyrie men from a hangar whose guardians had had no chance to throw this war vessel into action before the death was upon them.

"We flew across the Atlantic," Havig would tell me. "Headquarters was in . . . what had been . . . Wisconsin. Yes, they let me fetch my chronolog from where I'd hidden it, though I pleaded language difficulties to avoid telling them what it was. They themselves had had to cast about to zero in on the target date. That's a clumsy, lifespan-consuming process, which probably helps account for the dearth of travelers they found, and certainly explains their own organization's reluctance to make long temporal journeys. Return was easier, because they'd erected a kind of big billboard in the ruins, on which an indicator was set daily to the correct date.

"In late twenty-first-century America, things were barely getting started. The camp and sheds were inside a stockade and had been attacked more than once by, uh, natives or marauders. From then we moved on uptime to when the Sachem had sent his expedition out to that Easter."

I do not know if my friend ever looked upon Jesus.

chapter 7

After a hundred-odd years, the establishment was considerable. Fertility was increasing in formerly tainted soil, thus letting population build up. Grainfields ripened across low hills, beneath a mild sky where summer clouds walked. Cultivation of timber had produced stands which made cupolas of darker green where birds nested and wind murmured. Roads were dirt, but laid out in a grid. Folk were about, busy. They had nothing except hand tools and animal-drawn machines; however, these were well-made. They looked much alike in their mostly homespun blue trousers and jackets—both sexes—and their floppy straw hats and clumsy shoes: weather-beaten and work-gnarled like any pre-industrial peasants, hair hacked off below the ears, men bearded; they were small by the standards of our time, and many had poor teeth or none. Yet they were infinitely better off than their ancestors of the Judgment.

They paused to salute the travelers, who rode on horseback from the airfield site, then immediately resumed their toil. An occasional pair of mounted soldiers, going by, drew sabers in a deferential but less servile gesture. They were uniformed in blue, wore steel helmets and breastplates, bore dagger at belt, bow and quiver and ax at croup, lance in rest with red pennon aflutter from the shaft, besides those swords.

"You seem to keep tight control," Havig said uneasily.

"What else?" Krasicki snapped. "Most of the world, including most of this continent, is still in a state of barbarism or savagery, where man survives at all. We can't manufacture what we can't get the materials and machinery for. The Mong are on the plains west and south of us. They would come in like a tornado, did we let down our defenses. Our troopers aren't overseeing the workers, they're guarding them against bandits. No, those people can thank the Eyrie for everything they do have."

The medieval-like pattern was repeated in town. Families did not occupy separate homes, they lived together near the stronghold and worked the land collectively. But while it looked reasonably clean, which was a welcome difference from the Middle Ages, the place had none of the medieval charm. Brick rows flanking asphalted streets were as monotonous as anything in the Victorian Midlands. Havig supposed that was because the need for quick though stout construction had taken priority over individual choice, and the economic surplus remained too small to allow replacing these barracks with real houses. If not— But he ought to give the Sachem the benefit of the doubt, till he knew more. . . . He saw one picturesque feature, a wooden building in a style which seemed half Asian, gaudily painted. Krasicki told him it was a temple, where prayers were said to Yasu and sacrifices made to that Oktai whom the Mong had brought.

"Give them their religion, make the priests cooperate, and you have them," he added.

Havig grimaced. "Where's the gallows?"

Krasicki gave him a startled glance. "We don't hold public hangings. What do you think we are?" After a moment: "What milksop measures do you imagine can pull anybody through years like these?"

The fortress loomed ahead. High, turreted brick walls enclosed several acres; a moat surrounded them in turn, fed by the river which watered this area. The architecture had the same stern functionality as that of the town. Flanking the gates, and up among the battlements, were heavy machine guns, doubtless salvaged from wreckage or brought piece by piece out of the past. Stuttering noises told Havig that a number of motor-driven generators were busy inside.

Sentries presented arms. A trumpet blew. Drawbridge planks clattered, courtyard flagstones resounded beneath horsehoofs.

Krasicki's group reined in. A medley of people hastened from every direction, babbling their excitement. Most, liveried, must be castle servants. Havig scarcely noticed. His attention was on one who thrust her way past them until she stood before him.

Enthusiasm blazed from her. He could barely follow the husky, accented voice: "Oktai's tail! You did find 'm!"

She was nearly as tall as he, sturdily built, with broad shoulders and hips, comparatively small bust, long smooth limbs. Her face bore high cheekbones, blunt nose, large mouth, good teeth save that two were missing. (He would learn they had been knocked out in a fight.) Her hair, thick and mahogany, was not worn in today's style, but waist-length, though now coiled in braids above barbarically large brass earrings. Her eyes were brown and slightly almond—some Indian or Asian blood—under the heavy brows; her skin, sun-tanned, was in a few places crossed by old scars. She wore a loose red tunic and kilt, laced boots, a Bowie knife, a revolver, a loaded cartridge belt, and, on a chain around her neck, the articulated skull of a weasel.

"Where 'ey from? You, yon!" Her forefinger stabbed at Havig. " 'E High Years, no?" A whoop of laughter. "You got aplen'y for tell me, trailmate!"

"The Sachem is waiting," Krasicki reminded her.

" 'Kay, I'll wait alike, but not 'e whole jokin' day, you hear?" And when Havig had dismounted, she flung arms around him and kissed him full on the lips. She smelled of sunshine, leather, sweat, smoke, and woman. Thus did he meet Leonce of the Glacier Folk, the Skula of Wahorn.

The office was the antechamber of a suite whose size and luxury it reflected. Oak paneling rose above a deep-gray, thick-piled carpet. Drapes by the windows were likewise furry and feelable: mink. Because of their massiveness, desk, chairs, and couch had been fashioned in this section of time; but the care lavished on them was in contrast to the austerity Havig had observed in other rooms opening on the hallways which took him here. Silver frames held some photographs. One was a period piece, a daguerreotype of a faded-looking woman in the dress of the middle nineteenth century. The rest were candid shots taken with an advanced camera, doubtless a miniature using a telescopic lens like his own. He recognized Cecil Rhodes, Bismarck, and a youthful Napoleon; he could not place the yellow-bearded man in a robe.

From this fifth floor of the main keep, the view showed wide across that complex of lesser buildings, that bustle of activity, which was the Eyrie, and across the land it ruled. Afternoon light slanted in long hot bars. The generator noise was a muted pecking.

"Let's have music, eh?" Caleb Wallis flipped the switches of a molecular recorder from shortly before the Judgment. Notes boomed forth. He lowered the volume but said: "That's right, a triumphal piece. Lord, I'm glad to have you, Havig!" The newcomer recognized the Entry of the Gods from *Das Rheingold.*

The rest of his group, including their guides, had been dismissed, not altogether untactfully, after a short interview had demonstrated what they were. "You're different," the Sachem said. "You're the one in a hundred we need worst. Here, want a cigar?"

"No, thanks, I don't smoke."

Wallis stood for a moment before he said, emphatically rather than loudly, "I am the founder and master of this nation. We must have discipline, forms of respect. I'm called 'sir.' "

Havig regarded him. Wallis was of medium height, blocky and powerful despite the paunch of middle life. His face was ruddy, somewhat flat-nosed, tufty-browed; gingery-gray muttonchop whiskers crossed upper lip and cheeks to join the hair which fringed his baldness. He wore a black uniform, silver buttons and insignia, goldwork on the collar, epaulets, ornate dagger, automatic pistol. But there was nothing ridiculous about him. He radiated assurance. His voice rolled deep and compelling, well-nigh hypnotic when he chose. His small pale eyes never wavered.

"You realize," Havig said at last, "this is all new and bewildering to me . . . sir."

"Sure! Sure!" Wallis beamed and slapped him on the back. "You'll catch on fast. You'll go far, my boy. No limit here, for a man who knows what he wants and has the backbone to go after it. And you're an American, too. An honest-to-God American, from when our country was herself. Mighty few like that among us."

He lowered himself behind the desk. "Sit down. No, wait a minute, see my liquor cabinet? I'll take two fingers of the bourbon. You help yourself to what you like."

Havig wondered why no provision for ice and soda and

the rest had been made. It should have been possible. He decided Wallis didn't use such additions and didn't care that others might.

Seated in an armchair, a shot of rum between his fingers, he gazed at the Sachem and ventured: "I can go into detail about my biography, sir, but I think that could more usefully wait till I know what the Eyrie . . . is."

"Right, right." Wallis nodded his big head and puffed on the stogie. Its smoke was acrid. "However, let's just get a few facts straight about you. Born in—1933, did you say? Ever let on to anybody what you are?" Havig checked the impulse to mention me. The knowledgeable questions snapped: "Went back as a young man to guide your childhood? Went on to improve your station in life, and then to search for other travelers?"

"Yes, sir."

"What do you think of your era?"

"Huh? Why, uh, well . . . we're in trouble. I've gone ahead and glimpsed what's in store. Sir."

"Because of decay, Havig. You understand that, don't you?" Intensity gathered like a thunderhead. "Civilized man turning against himself, first in war, later in moral sickness. The white man's empires crumbling faster than Rome's; the work of Clive, Bismarck, Rhodes, McKinley, Lyautey, all Indian fighters and Boers, everything that'd been won, cast out in a single generation; pride of race and heritage gone; traitors—Bolsheviks and international Jews—in the seats of power, preaching to the ordinary white man that the wave of the future was black. I've seen that, studying your century. You, living in it, have you seen?"

Havig bristled. "I've seen what prejudice, callousness, and stupidity bring about. The sins of the fathers are very truly visited on the sons."

Wallis chose to ignore the absence of an honorific. Indeed, he smiled and grew soothing: "I know. I know. Don't get me wrong. Plenty of colored men are fine, brave fellows—Zulus, for instance, or Apache Indians to take a different race, or Japs to take still another. Any travelers we may find among them will get their chance to occupy the same honored position as all our proven time agents do, as you will yourself, I'm sure. Shucks, I admire your Israelis, what I've heard about them. A mongrel people, racially no relation to the Hebrews of the Bible, but tough fighters and clever. No, I'm just talking about the need for everybody to keep his own identity and pride. And I'm only mad at those classes it's fair to call niggers, redskins, Chinks, kikes, wops, you know what I mean. Plenty of pure-blooded whites among them, I'm sorry to say, who've either lost heart or have outright sold themselves to the enemy."

Havig forced himself to remember that that basic attitude was common, even respectable in the Sachem's birth-century. Why, Abraham Lincoln had spoken of the inborn inferiority of the Negro. . . . He didn't suppose Wallis ordered crucifixions.

"Sir," he said with much care, "I suggest we avoid argument till we've made the terms of our thinking clear to each other. That may take a lot of effort. Meanwhile we can better discuss practical matters."

"Right, right," Wallis rumbled. "You're a brain, Havig. A man of action, too, though maybe within limits. But I'll be frank, brains are what we need most at this stage, especially if they have scientific training, realistic philosophies." He waved the cigar. "Take that haul today from Jerusalem. Typical! The Brabanter and the Greek we can probably train up to be useful fighting men, scouts, auxiliaries on time expeditions, that sort of thing. But the rest—" He clicked his tongue. "I don't know. Maybe, at most, ferrymen, fetching stuff from the past. And I can only hope the woman'll be a breeder."

"What?" Havig started half out of his chair. It leaped inside him. "We can have children?"

"With each other, yes. In the course of a hundred years we've proved that." Wallis guffawed. "Not with non-travelers, no, not ever. We've proved that even oftener. How'd you like a nice little servant girl to warm your bed tonight, hm? Or we have slaves, taken on raids—and don't go moralistic on me. Their gangs would've done the same to us, and if we didn't bring prisoners back here and tame them, rather than cut their throats, they and their brats would go on making trouble along our borders." His mood had reverted to serious. "Quite a shortage of traveler women here, as you'd expect, and not all of them willing or able to become mothers. But those who do—the kids are ordinary, Havig. The gift is not inherited."

Considering the hypothesis he had made (how far ago on his multiply twisted world line?), the younger man was unsurprised. If two such sets of chromosomes could interact to make a life, it must be because the resonances (?) which otherwise barred fertility were canceled out.

"Well, then, no use trying to breed a race from ourselves," Wallis continued wistfully. "Oh, we do give our kids educations, preference, leadership jobs when they're grown. I have to allow that, it being one thing which helps keep my agents loyal to me. But frankly, confidentially, I'm often hard put to find handsome-looking posts where somebody's get can do no harm. Because the parents are time travelers, it doesn't follow they're not chuckleheads fit only to bring forth more chuckleheads. No, we're a kind of aristocracy in these parts, I won't deny, but we can't keep it hereditary for very long. I wouldn't want that anyway."

Havig asked softly: "What do you want, sir?"

Wallis put aside his cigar and drink, as if his next words required the piety of folded hands on the desk before him. "To restore civilization. Why else did God make our kind?"

"But—in the future—I've glimpsed—"

"The Maurai Federation?" Fury flushed the wide countenance. A fist thudded down. "How much of it have you seen? Damn little, right? I've explored that epoch, Havig. You'll be taken to learn for yourself. I tell you, they're a bunch of Kanaka-white-nigger-Chink-Jap mongrels who'll come to power—are starting to come to power while we sit here—for no other reason than that they were less hard-hit. They'll work, and fight, and bribe, and connive to dominate the world, only so they can put bridle and saddle on the human race in general, the white race in particular, and stop progress forever. You'll see! You'll see!"

He leaned back, breathed hard, swallowed his whiskey, and stated: "Well, they won't succeed. For three-four centuries, yes, I'm afraid men will have to bear their yoke. But afterward— That's what the Eyrie is for, Havig. To prepare an afterward."

"I was born in 1853, upstate New York," the Sachem related. "My father was a poor storekeeper and a strict Baptist. My mother—that's her picture." He indicated the gentle, ineffectual face upon the wall, and for an instant a tenderness broke through. "I was the last of seven children who lived. So Father hadn't a lot of time or energy to spare for me, especially since the oldest boy was his favorite. Well, that taught me at an early age how to look out for myself and keep my mouth shut. Industry and thrift, too. I went to Pittsburgh when I was officially seventeen, knowing by then how much of the future was there. My older self had worked closer with me than I gather yours did. But then, I always knew I had a destiny."

"How did you make your fortune, sir?" Havig inquired. He was interested as well as diplomatic.

"Well, my older self joined the Forty-niners in California. He didn't try for more than a good stake, just enough to invest for a proper profit in sutlering when he skipped on to the War between the States. Next he had me run over his time track, and when I came back to Pittsburgh the rest was easy. You can't call 'em land speculations when you know what's due to happen, right? I sold short at the proper point in '73, and after the panic was in a position to buy up distressed property that would become valuable for coal and oil. Bought into railroads and steel mills, too, in spite of trouble from strikers and anarchists and suchlike trash. By 1880, my real age about thirty-five, I figured I'd made my pile and could go on to the work for which God had created me."

Solemnly: "I've left my father's faith. I guess most time travelers do. But I still believe in a God who every now and then calls a particular man to a destiny."

And then Wallis laughed till his belly jiggled and exclaimed: "But my, oh, my, ain't them highfalutin words for a plain old American! It's not glamour and glory, Havig, except in the history books. It's hard, grubby detail work, it's patience and self-denial and being willing to learn from the mistakes more than the successes. You see how I'm not young any more, and my plans barely started to blossom, let alone bear fruit. The doing, though, the doing, that's the thing, that's to be alive!"

He held out his empty glass. "Refill this," he said. "I don't ordinarily drink much, but Lord, how I've wanted to talk to somebody both new and bright! We have several shrewd boys, like Krasicki, but they're foreigners, except a couple of Americans who I've gotten so used to I can tell you beforehand what they'll say to any remark of mine. Go on, pour for me, and yourself, and let's chat awhile."

Presently Havig could ask: "How did you make your first contacts, sir?"

"Why, I hired me a lot of agents, throughout most of the nineteenth century, and had them go around placing advertisements in papers and magazines and almanacs, or spreading a word of mouth. They didn't say 'time traveler,' of course, nor know what I really wanted. That wording was very careful. Not that I made it myself. I'm no writer. Brains are what a man of action hires. I hunted around and found me a young Englishman in the '90's, starting out as an author, a gifted fellow even if he was kind of a socialist. I wanted somebody late in the period, to avoid, um-m, anticipations, you see? He got interested in my, ha, 'hypothetical proposition,' and for a few guineas wrote me some clever things. I offered him more money but he said he'd rather have the free use of that time travel idea instead."

Havig nodded; a tingle went along his nerves. "Some such thought occurred to me, sir. But, well, I hadn't your singlemindedness. I definitely don't seem to have accumulated anything like your fortune. And besides, in my period, time travel was so common a fictional theme, I was afraid of publicity. At best, it seemed I'd merely attract cranks."

"I got those!" Wallis admitted. "A few genuine, even: I mean travelers whose gift had made them a little tetched, or more than a little. Remember, a dimwit or a yokel, if he isn't scared green of what's happened to him and never does it again—or doesn't want to travel outside the horizon he knows—or doesn't get taken by surprise and murdered for a witch—he'll hide what he is, and that'll turn him strange. Or say he's a street urchin, why shouldn't he make himself rich as a burglar or a bookmaker, something like that, then retire to the life of Riley? Or say he's an Injun on the reservation, he can impress the devil out of his tribe and make them support him, but they aren't about to tell the palefaces, are they? And so on and so on. Hopeless cases. As for one like me, who is smart and ambitious, why, he'll lay low same as you and I did, won't he? Often, I'm afraid, too low for any of us to find."

"How . . . how many did you gather?"

"Sir?"

"I'm sorry. Sir."

Wallis gusted a breath. "Eleven. Out of a whole blooming century, eleven in that original effort." He ticked them off. "Austin Caldwell the best of the lot. A fuzzy-cheeked frontier scout when he came to my office; but he's turned into quite a man, quite a man. He it was who nicknamed me the Sachem. I kind of liked that, and let it stick.

"Then a magician and fortuneteller in a carnival; a professional gambler; a poor-white Southern girl. That was the Americans. Abroad, we found a Bavarian soldier; an investigator for the Inquisition, which was still going on in Spain, you may know; a female Jew cultist in Hungary; a student in Edinburgh, working his heart out trying to learn from books what he might be; a lady milliner in Paris, who went off into time for her designs; a young peasant couple in Austria. We were lucky with those last, by the way. They'd found each other—maybe the only pair of travelers who were ever born neighbors—and had their first child, and wouldn't have left if the baby weren't small enough to carry.

"What a crew! You can imagine the problems of language and transportation and persuading and everything."

"No more than those?" Havig felt appalled.

"Yes, about as many, but unusable. Cracked, like I told you, or too dull, or crippled, or scared to join us, or whatever. One strapping housewife who refused to leave her husband. I thought of abducting her—the cause is bigger than her damn comfort—but what's the good of an unwilling traveler? A man, maybe you could threaten his kin and get service out of him. Women are too cowardly."

Havig remembered a flamboyant greeting in the courtyard, but held his peace.

"Once I had my first disciples, I could expand," Wallis told him. "We could explore wider and in more detail, learning better what needed to be done and how. We could establish funds and bases at key points of . . . m-m . . . yes, space-time. We could begin to recruit more, mainly from different centuries but a few additional from our own. Finally we could pick our spot for the Eyrie, and take command of the local people for a labor supply. Poor starved harried wretches, they welcomed warlords who brought proper guns and seed corn!"

Havig tugged his chin. "May I ask why you chose that particular place and year to start your nation, sir?"

"Sure, ask what you want," Wallis said genially. "Chances are I'll answer. . . . I thought of the past. You can see from yonder picture I've been clear back to Charlemagne, testing my destiny. It's too long a haul, though. And even in an unexplored section like pre-Columbian America, we'd risk leaving traces for archaeologists to discover. Remember, there could be Maurai time travelers, and what we've got to have is surprise. Right now, these centuries, feudalisms like ours are springing up everywhere, recovery is being made, and we take care not to look unique. Our subjects know we have powers, of course, but they call us magicians and children of the Those—gods and spirits. By the time that story's filtered past the wild people, it's only a vague rumor of still another superstitious cult."

Havig appreciated the strategy. "As far as I've been able

to find out, sir, which isn't much," he said, "the, uh, the Maurai culture is right now forming in the Pacific basin. Anybody from its later stages, coming downtime, would doubtless be more interested in that genesis than in the politics of obscure, impoverished barbarians."

"You do your Americans an injustice," Wallis reproved him. "You're right, of course, from the Maurai standpoint. But actually, our people have had a run of bad luck."

There was some truth in that, Havig must agree. Parts of Oceania had been too unimportant for overdevelopment or for strikes by the superweapons; and those enormous waters were less corrupted than seas elsewhere, more quickly self-cleansed after man became again a rare species. Yet the inhabitants were no simple and simpering dwellers in Eden. Books had been printed in quantities too huge, distributed over regions too wide, for utter loss of any significant information. To a lesser degree, the same was true of much technological apparatus.

North America, Europe, parts of Asia and South America, fewer parts of Africa, hit bottom because they were overextended. Let the industrial-agricultural-medical complexes they had built be paralyzed for the shortest of whiles, and people would begin dying by millions. The scramble of survivors for survival would bring everything else down in wreck.

Now even in such territories, knowledge was preserved: by an oasis of order here, a half-religiously venerated community there. At last, theoretically, it could diffuse to the new barbarians, who would pass it on to the new savages . . . theoretically. Practice said otherwise. The old civilization had stripped the world too bare.

You could, for example, log a virgin forest, mine a virgin Mesabi, pump a virgin oil field, by primitive methods. Using your gains from this, you could go on to build a larger and more sophisticated plant capable of more intricate operations. As resources dwindled, it could replace lumber with plastics, squeeze iron out of taconite, scour the entire planet for petroleum.

But by the time of the Judgment, this had *been* done. That combination of machines, trained personnel, well-heeled consumers and taxpayers, went under and was not to be reconstructed.

The data needed for an industrial restoration could be found. The natural materials could not.

"Don't you think, sir," Havig dared say, "by their development of technological alternatives, the Maurai and their allies will do a service?"

"Up to a point, yes. I have to give the bastards that," Wallis growled. His cigar jabbed the air. "But that's as far as it goes. Far enough to put them hard in the saddle, and not an inch more. We're learning about their actual suppression of new developments. You will likewise."

He seemed to want to change the subject, for he continued: "Anyhow, as to our organization here. My key men haven't stuck around in uninterrupted normal time, and I less. We skip ahead—overlapping—to keep leadership continuous. And we're doing well. Things snowball for us, in past, present, and future alike.

"By now we've hundreds of agents, plus thousands of devoted commoners. We rule over what used to be a couple of whole states, though of course our traffic is more in time than space. Mainly we govern through common-born deputies. When you can travel along the lifespan of a promising boy, you can make a fine and trusty man out of him—especially when he knows he'll never have any secrets from you, nor any safety.

"But don't get me wrong. I repeat, we aren't monsters or parasites. Sometimes we do have to get rough. But our aim is always to put the world back on the path God laid out for it."

He leaned forward. "And we will," he almost whispered. "I've traveled beyond. A thousand years hence, I've seen—

"Are you with us?"

chapter 8

"By and large, the next several months were good," Havig would relate (would have related) to me. "However, I stayed cautious. For instance, I hedged on giving out exact biographical data. And I passed the chronolog off as a radionic detector and transmitter, built in case visitors to the past had such gear in use. Wallis said he doubted they did and lost interest. I found a hiding place for it. If they were the kind of people in the Eyrie I hoped they were, they'd understand when I finally confessed my hesitation about giving them something this helpful."

"What made you wary?" I asked.

His thin features drew into a scowl. "Oh . . . minor details at first. Like Wallis' whole style. Though, true, I didn't have a proper chance to get acquainted, because he soon hopped forward to the following year. Think how that lengthens and strengthens power!"

"Unless his subordinates conspire against him meanwhile," I suggested.

He shook his head. "Not in this case. He knows who's certainly loyal, among both his agents and his hand-reared commoners. A hard core of travelers shuttles in and out through time with him, on a complicated pattern which always has one of them clearly in charge.

"Besides, how'd you brew a conspiracy among meek commoner farmers and laborers, arrogant commoner soldiers and officials, or the travelers themselves? They're a wildly diverse and polyglot band, those I met in the castle and those stationed in outlying areas. Nearly all from post-medieval Western civilizations—"

"Why?" I wondered. "Surely the rest of history has possibilities in proportion."

"Yeah, and Wallis said he did mean to extend the range of his recruiters. But the difficulties of long temporal trips, language and culture barriers, training whomever you brought back, seemed too great thus far. His Jerusalem search was an experiment, and aside from me had a disappointing result."

Havig shrugged. "To return to the main question," he said, "American English is the Eyrie's official language, which everybody's required to learn. But even so, with most I could never communicate freely. Besides accents, our minds were too different. From my angle, the majority of them were ruffians. From theirs, I was a sissy, or else too sly-acting for comfort. And they had, they have their mutual jealousies and suspicions. Simply being together doesn't stop them regarding each other as Limeys, Frogs, Boches, Guineas, the hereditary enemy. How would you give them a common cause?

"And, finally, why on Earth should they mutiny? Only a few are idealists of any kind; that's a rare quality, remember. But we lived—they live—like fighting cocks. The best of food, drink, time-imported luxuries, servants, bed partners, sports, liberal furloughs to the past, if reasonable precautions are observed, and ample pocket money provided. The work isn't hard. Those who need it get training in what history and technology are appropriate to their talents. The able-bodied learn commando skills. The rest become clerks, temporal porters, administrators, or researchers if they have the brains for it. That was our routine, by no means a dull one. The work itself was fascinating—or would be, I knew, as soon as my superiors decided I was properly trained. Think: a scout in time!

"No, on the whole I had no serious complaints. At first."

"You don't seem to have found your associates really congenial, however," I said.

"A few I did," he replied. "Wallis himself could charm as well as domineer: in his fashion, a spellbinding conversationalist, what with everything he'd experienced. His top lieutenant, Austin Caldwell, gray now but whipcord-tough still, crack shot and horseman, epic whiskey drinker, he had the same size fund of stories to draw on, plus more humor; in addition, he was a friendly soul who went out of his way to make my beginnings easier. Reuel Orrick, that former carnival magician, a delightful old rogue. Jerry Jennings, hardly more than an English schoolboy, desperately trying to find a new dream after his old ones broke apart in the trenches, 1918. A few more. And then Leonce." He smiled, though it was a haunted smile. "Especially Leonce."

They rode forth upon a holiday, soon after his arrival. He had barely gotten moved into his two-room castle apartment, and as yet had few possessions. She presented him with a bearskin rug and a bottle of Glenlivet from downtime. He wasn't sure if it was mere cordiality, like that which some others showed, or what. Her manner baffled him more than her dialect. A lusty kiss, within five minutes of first sight—then casual cheerfulness, and she sat by a different man practically every mess— But Havig found too much else to occupy his mind, those early days.

The proffered concubine was not among them. He didn't like the idea of a woman being ordered to his couch. This was an extra reason to welcome Leonce's invitation to a picnic, when they got their regular day off.

Bandits had been thoroughly suppressed in the vicinity, and mounted patrols assured they would not slip back. It was safe to go out unescorted. The pair carried pistols only as a badge which none but their kind were allowed.

Leonce chose the route, several miles through fields dreamy beneath the morning sun, until a trail left the road for a timberlot big enough to gladden Havig with memories of Morgan Woods. A scent of new-cut hay yielded to odors of leaf and humus. It was warm, but a breeze ruffled foliage, stroked the skin, made sunflecks dance in shadow. Squirrels streaked and chattered over branches. Hoofs beat slowly, muscles moved at leisure between human thighs.

On the way she had eagerly questioned him. He was glad to oblige, within the broad circle drawn by discretion. What normal man does not like to tell an attractive woman about himself? Especially when to her his background is fabulous! The language fence toppled. She had not been here long either, less than a year even if temporal trips were reckoned in. But she could speak his English fairly well by now when she wasn't excited; and his talented ear began to pick up hers.

"From the High Years!" she breathed, leaned in her stirrups and squeezed his arm. Her hands bore calluses.

"Uh, what do you mean by that?" he asked. "Shortly before the Judgment?"

"Ay-yeh, when men reached for moon an' stars an'—an' ever'thing." He realized that, despite her size and brashness, she was quite young. The tilted eyes shone upon him from beneath the ruddy hair, which today hung in pigtails tied with ribbons.

When we doomed ourselves to become our own execu-

tioners, he thought. But he didn't want to croak about that. "You look as if you come from a hopeful period," he said.

She made a *moue*, but at once grew pensive, cradled chin in fist and frowned at her horse's ears, until: "Well, yes an' no. Same's for you, I reckon."

"Won't you explain? I've heard you're from uptime of here, but I don't know more."

When she nodded, red waves of light ran over her mane. " 'Bout 'nother hun'erd 'n' fifty year. Glacier Folk."

After they entered the woods they could not ride abreast. Guiding, she led the way. He admired her shape from behind, and her grace in the saddle; and often she turned her head to flash him a grin while she talked.

Her homeland he identified as that high and beautiful country which he had known as Glacier and Waterton Parks and on across the Bitterroot Range. Today her ancestors were in its eastern part, having fled from Mong who conquered the plains for their own herds and ranches. Already they were hunters and trappers more than smallhold farmers, raiders of the lowland enemy, elsewhere traders who brought furs, hides, ores, slaves in exchange for foodstuffs and finished products. Not that they were united; feuds among families, clans, tribes would range for generations.

But as their numbers and territory expanded, a measure of organization would evolve. Leonce tried to describe: "Look, you, I'm o' the Ranyan kin, who belong in the Wahorn troop. A kin's a . . . a gang o' families who share the same blood. A troop meets four times a year, under its Sherf, who leads 'em in killin' cattle for Gawd an' Oktai an' the rest o' what folk here-aroun' call the Those. Then they talk about things, an' judge quarrels, an' maybe vote on laws—the grownups who could come, men an' women both." Merriment pealed. "Ha! So we per-ten'. Mainly it's to meet, gossip, dicker, swap, gorge, booze, joke, show off . . . you know?"

"I think I do," Havig answered. Some such institution was common in primitive societies.

"In later time," she continued, "Sherfs, an' whatever troop people can go 'long, been meetin' likewise once a year, in the Congers. The Jinral runs that show: first-born to the line o' Injun Samal, in the Rover kin who belong to no troop. It'd be a blood-flood, that many diff'rent kin together, or would've been at the start, 'cep' it's at Lake Pendoray, which is peace-holy."

Havig nodded. The wild men became less wild as the advantages of law and order grew in their minds—no doubt after Injun Samal had knocked the heads of their chieftains together.

"When I left, things were perty quiet," Leonce said. "The Mong were gone, an' we traded of'ner'n we fought with the new lowlanders, who're strong an' rich. More 'n' more we were copyin' 'em." She sighed. "A hun'erd years after me, I've learned, the Glacier Folk are in the Nor'wes' Union. I don't want to go back."

"You seem to have had a rough life just the same."

"Ay-yeh. Could'a been worse. An' what the jabber, I got plen'y life to go. . . . Here we are."

They tied their horses in a small meadow which fronted on a brook. Trees behind it and across the swirling, bubbling brown water stood fair against heaven; grass grew thick and soft, starred with late wildflowers. Leonce unpacked the lunch she had commanded to be prepared, a hearty enough collection of sandwiches and fruit that Havig doubted he could get around his whole share. Well, they wanted a rest and a drink first anyway. He joined her, shoulder to shoulder; they leaned back against a bole and poured wine into silver cups.

"Go on," he reminded. "I want to hear about you."

Her lashes fluttered. He observed the tiny freckles across cheekbones and nose. "Aw, nothin' nex' to you, Jack."

"Please. I'm interested."

She laughed for delight. Yet the tale she gave him, in matter-of-fact phrases that begged no sympathy, had its grimness.

In most respects a Glacier family, which turned such fangs to the outer world, was affectionate and close-knit. An earlier tradition of equality between the sexes had never died there, or else had revived in an age when any woman might at any moment have to hunt or do battle. Of course, some specialization existed. Thus men took the heaviest manual labor, women the work demanding most patience. Men always offered the sacrifices; but what Leonce called skuling was a prerogative of the female only, if she showed a bent for it. "Foreknowin'," she explained. "Unravelin' dreams. Readin' an writin'. Healin' some kinds o' sickness. Drivin' black fogs out o' heads. Sendin' ghosts back where they belong. That kind o' job. An' . . . m-m-m . . . ways to trick the eye, fool the mind—you know?"

But hers was no sleight-of-hand or ritual performance. No older self came to warn that child about keeping secrecy.

Her father was (would be) Wolfskin-Jem, a warrior of note. He died fighting off an attack whipped up by the Dafy kin, ostensibly to kill the "thing" which had been born to him, actually to end a long-smoldering feud. But his wife Onda escaped with their children, to find refuge among the Donnal troop. There followed years of guerrilla war and intrigue, before the Ranyans got allies and made their crushing comeback. Leonce, as a spy through time, played a key role. Inevitably, she became the new Skula.

Among friends she was regarded initially with respect, not

dread. She learned and practiced the normal skills, the normal sports. But her gift marked her out, and awe grew around her as her ability did. From Onda she learned to be sparing of it. (Also, despite stoic fatalism, it hurt to foreknow the misfortunes of those she cared about.) Nevertheless, having such a Skula, Wahorn waxed mighty.

And Leonce, ever more, became lonely. Her siblings married and moved away, leaving her and Onda by themselves in Jem's old lodge. Both took lovers, as was the custom of unwedded women, but none of Leonce's sought marriage, if only because she seemed to be barren, and gradually they stopped seeking her at all. Former playmates sought her for help and advice, never pleasure. Reaching after comradeship, she insisted on accompanying and fighting in raids on the lowlands. The kindred of those who fell shunned her and mumbled questions about why the Skula had allowed deaths that surely one of her power could have forbidden—or did she *want* them—? Then Onda died.

Not much later, Eyrie scouts tracked down a far-flung rumor to the source, herself. She welcomed them with tears and jubilation. Wahorn would never see her again.

"My God," Havig laid an arm around her. "You have had it cruel."

"Aw, was plen'y good huntin', skiin', feastin', singin', lots o' jokin' once I'd gotten here." She had downed a quantity of wine. It made her breath fragrant as she nuzzled him. "I don't sing bad. Wanna hear?"

"Sure."

She bounded to fetch an instrument like a dwarf guitar from a saddlebag, and was back in a second. "I play a bone flute too, but can't sing 'long o' that, hm? Here's a song I made myself. I used to pass a lot o' lone-time makin' songs."

A little to his astonishment, she was excellent. "*—Ride*

w'ere strides a rattle o' rocks,/Thunder 'e sun down t' dance on your lance—" What he could follow raised gooseflesh on him.

"Wow," he said low when she had finished. "What else do you do?"

"Well, I can read an' write, sort o'. Play chess. Rules changed some from home to here, but I take mos' games anyhow. An' Austin taught me poker; I win a lot. An' I joke."

"Hm?"

She grinned and leaned into his embrace. "Figgered we'd joke after lunch, Jack, honeybee," she murmured. "but w'y not 'fore *an'* after? Hm-m-m-m?"

He discovered, with glee which turned to glory, that one more word would in the course of generations change its meaning.

•

"Yeah," he told me. "We moved in together. It lasted till . . . I left. Several months. Mostly they were fine. I really liked that girl."

"Not loved, evidently," I observed.

"N-n-no. I suppose not. Though what is love, anyway? Doesn't it have so infinitely many kinds and degrees and mutations and quantum jumps that— Never mind." He stared into the night which filled the windows of the room where we sat. "We had our fights, roof-shattering quarrels she'd end by striking me and taunting me because I wouldn't strike back, till she rushed out. Touchy as a fulminate cap, my Leonce. The reconciliations were every bit as wild." He rubbed weary eyes. "Not suitable to my temperament, eh, Doc? And I'll admit I was jealous, my jealousy brought on a lot of the trouble. She'd slept with many agents, and commoners for that matter, before I arrived, not to mention her highland lads earlier. She went on doing it too, not often, but if she particularly liked a man, this was her way to be kind and get closer to him. I had the same freedom, naturally, with other women, but . . . I . . . didn't . . . want it."

"Why didn't she get pregnant by an, uh, agent?"

His mouth twitched upward. "When she heard in the Eyrie what the situation was, she insisted on being taken to the last High Years, partly for a look around, like me going to Pericles' Greece or Michelangelo's Italy, but also to get a reversible-sterilization shot. She wanted children in due course, when she felt ready to settle down—Glacier wives are chaste, it seems—but that wasn't yet and meanwhile she enjoyed sex, same as she enjoyed everything else in life. Judas priest, what a lay she was!"

"If she mainly stayed with you, however, there must have been a strong attraction on both sides," I said.

"There was. I've tried, as near as my privacy fetish will let me, to tell you what held me to her. From Leonce's side . . . hard to be sure. How well did we actually know each other? How well have any man and woman ever? My learning and, yes, intelligence excited her. She had a fine mind, hit-or-miss-educated but fine. And, I'll be frank, I doubtless had the top IQ in the Eyrie. Then, too, I suppose we felt the attraction of opposites. She called me sweet and gentle—not patronizingly, because I did do pretty well in games and exercises, being from a better-nourished era than average—but I was no stark mountaineer or roughneck Renaissance mercenary."

Again ghosts dwelt in his smile. "On the whole," he said, "she gave me the second-best part of my life, so far and I think probably forever. I'll always be grateful to her, for that and for what followed."

Havig's suspicions developed slowly. He fought them. But piece by piece, the evidence accumulated that something was being withheld from him. It lay in the evasion of certain topics, the brushoff of certain questions, whether with Austin Caldwell's embarrassment, or Coenraad van Leuven's brusque "I may not say what I have been told," or Reuel Orrick's changing the subject and proceeding to get weeping drunk, or the mild "In God's good time all shall be revealed to you, my son" of Padre Diego the Inquisitor, or an obscene command to shut up from various warrior types.

He was not alone in this isolation. Of those others whom he approached about it, most were complaisant, whether from prudence or indifference. But young Jerry Jennings exclaimed, "By Jove, you're right!"

So did Leonce, in more pungent words. Then after a moment she said: "Well, they can't give us new 'uns ever'thing in a single chaw, can they?"

"Coenraad's as new as I am," he protested. "Newer than you."

Her curiosity piqued, she found her own methods of investigation. They were not what you'd think. She could match a tough, woman-despising man-at-arms goblet for goblet till he was sodden and pliable, while her head remained ice-clear. She could trap a sober person by an adroit question; it helped having been a shaman. And she appalled Havig by whispering to him at night, amidst schoolgirl giggles, how she had done what was strictly forbidden without permission, slipped into different periods of the Eyrie's existence to snoop, pry, and eavesdrop.

She concluded: "Near's I can learn, ol' Wallis's jus' feared you an' 'em like you might get mad at what some o' the agents do in some times an' places. Anyhow, till you're more used to the *i*-dear."

"I was arriving at the same notion myself," Havig said bleakly. "I've seen what earlier ages are like, what personalities they breed. The travelers who respond to his come-ons, or make themselves conspicuous enough for his searchers to hear about, are apt to be the bold—which in most cases means the ruthless. Coming here doesn't change them."

"Seems like orders is, you got to be led slow to the truth. I s'pose I'm only kep' from it 'cause of bein' by you." She kissed him. " 'S'kay, darlya."

"You mean you'd condone robbery and—"

"Hush. We got to use who we can get. Maybe they do be rough. Your folk, they never were?"

Sickly, he remembered how . . . from Wounded Knee to My Lai, and before and after . . . he never disowned his nation. For where and when—if it had not abdicated all responsibility for the future—existed a better society?

(Denmark, maybe? Well, the Danes boasted about Viking ancestors, who were comfortably distant in time, but stayed notably silent about what happened during the slave uprising in the Virgin Islands, 1848, or less directly in Greenland. By 1950 or so, of course, they were free to relax into a smugness shared by the Swedes, who had not only traded with Hitler but let his troop trains roll through their land. And yet these were countries which did much good in the world.)

" 'Sides," Leonce said candidly, "the weak go down, 'less they're lucky an' got somebody strong to guard 'em. An' in the end, come the Ol' Man, we're all weak." She thought for a minute. "Could be," she mused, "was I undyin', I'd never kill more'n a spud, an' it only for food. But I will die. I'm in the game too. So're you, darlya. Let's play for the best score we can make, hm?"

He pondered long upon that.

"But if nothing else," he told me, and I heard his anguish, "I had to try and make certain the gold was worth more than the tailings."

"Or the end could justify the means?" I responded.

"Sure, I follow. To say it never does is a counsel of perfection. In the real world, you usually must choose the lesser evil. Speaking as an old doctor—no—well, yes, I'll admit I've given my share of those shots which end the incurable pain; and sometimes the choice has been harder. Go on, please do."

"I'd been promised a survey of the Maurai epoch," he said, "so I could satisfy myself it was, at best, a transition period, whose leaders became tyrants and tried to freeze the world. So I could agree that, when the Maurai hegemony began to crumble—perhaps hastened by our subversion—we ought to intervene, seize power, help turn men back toward achievement and advancement."

"Not openly, surely," I objected. "That, the sudden mass appearance of time travelers, would produce headlines nobody could mistake."

"True, true. We were to spend centuries building our strength in secret, till we were ready to act in disguise. It wasn't made clear exactly what disguise; but it was admitted that information was still sparse, because of the usual difficulties. Besides, I heard long philosophical arguments from guys like Padre Diego, about free will and the rest. I thought the logic stank, but said nothing."

"Had, um, Leonce already been taken uptime?"

"Yes. That's why she basically favored Wallis, in spite of her occasional naughtinesses. She told me about a world where progress had been made, more and more peaceful-looking for a long span of history. Except she could not agree this was necessarily progress. Granted, that world did have fleets of efficient sailing ships and electric-powered dirigibles, ocean ranches, solar energy screens charging accumulators, widescale use of bacterial fuel cells which ran off the wastes of living organisms, new developments in both theoretical and applied science, especially biology—"

He stopped for breath and I tried to inject a light note: "Don't tell me your pet Valkyrie used such terms!"

"No, no." He continued earnest. "I'm anticipating what I saw or had explained to me. Her impressions were more general. But she had that huntress and sorceress knack of close observation. She was quite able to trace the basic course of events."

"Which was?"

"Men did not go on to any fresh peak. Instead, what they reached was a plateau, where they stayed. The bio-technological culture didn't improve further, it merely spread further.

"That was scarcely her ideal of the High Years restored, or Wallis's of unlimited growth and accomplishment.

"The tour skimmed fast through a later phase of what appeared to be retrogression and general violence. Eyrie agents don't dare explore it in detail till they have a larger and stronger organization. Nor can they understand what lies beyond. It seems peaceful once more, but it's not comprehensible. From the glimpse I had, I'm prepared to believe that."

"What was it like?" I asked. "Can you tell me?"

"Very little." His tone fell rough. "I haven't time. Sound strange, coming from me? Well, it's true. I'm a fugitive, remember."

"I gather your trip uptime did not remove your skepticism about Wallis's intentions," I said, more calmly than I felt. "Why?"

He ran his fingers through his blond, sweat-dankened hair. "I'm a child of this century," he replied. "Think, Doc. Recall how intelligent men like, well, Bertrand Russell or Henry Wallace took extensive tours of Stalin's Russia, and came home to report that it did have its problems but those had been exaggerated and were entirely due to extraneous factors and a benevolent government was coping with everything. Don't forget, either, the chances are that most of their guides *did* think this, and were in full sincerity obeying instructions to shield a foreign visitor from what he might misinterpret." His grin was unpleasant. "Maybe the curse of my life is that I've lost the will to believe."

"You mean," I said, "you wondered if the world really would benefit from the rule of the Eyrie? And if maybe the Maurai were being slandered, you being shown nothing except untypical badness?"

"No, not exactly that, either. Depends on interpretation and—oh, here's a prime example."

Not every recruit was given as thorough a tour as Havig. Plainly Wallis deemed him to be both of particular potential value and in particular need of convincing.

By doubling back and forth through chronology, he got a look at documents in ultra-secret files. (He could puzzle them out, since Ingliss was an official second language of the Federation and spelling had changed less than pronunciation.) One told how scientists in Hinduraj had clandestinely developed a hydrogen-fusion generator which would end Earth's fuel shortage, and the Maurai had as clandestinely learned of it, sabotaged it, and applied such politico-economic pressures that the truth never became public.

The motive given was that this revolutionary innovation would have upset the Pax. Worse, it would have made possible a rebirth of the ancient rapacious machine culture, which the planet could not endure.

And yet . . . uptime of the Maurai dominion, Havig saw huge silent devices and energies . . . and men, beasts, grass, trees, stars bright through crystalline air. . . .

"Were the Pacific sociologists and admirals sincere in their belief?" he said in a harsh whisper. "Or were they only preserving their top-dog status? Or both, or neither, or what?

"And is that farther future good? It could be a smooth-running monstrosity, you know, or it could be undermining the basis of all life's existence, or—How could I tell?"

"What did you ask your guides?" I responded.

"Those same questions. The leader was Austin Caldwell, by the way, an honest man, hard as the Indians who once hunted his scalp but nevertheless honest."

"What did he tell you?"

"To stop my goddam quibbling and trust the Sachem. The Sachem had done grand thus far, hadn't he? The Sachem had studied and thought about these matters; he didn't pretend to know everything himself, but we'd share the wisdom he was gathering as it became ready, and he would lead us onto the right paths.

"As for me, Austin said, I'd better remember how slow and awkward it was, getting around like this, having to return across centuries whenever we needed transportation to a new area. I'd already had as much lifespan and trouble spent on me as I was worth, anyhow, at my present stage of development. If I couldn't accept the discipline that an outfit must have which is embarked on dangerous endeavors—well, I was free to resign, but I'd better never show my hide near the Eyrie again.

"What could I do? I apologized and came back with them."

chapter 9

He was given a couple of days off, which he spent regaining his spirits in Leonce's company. The period of his training and indoctrination had brought winter's chances for old-fashioned sports outdoors and indoors. Thereafter he was assigned to reread Wallis's history of the future, ponder it in the light of what he had witnessed, and discuss any questions with Waclaw Krasicki, who was the most scholarly of the garrison's current directorate.

The Sachem admitted he was far from omniscient. But he had seen more than anyone else, on repeated expeditions with differing escorts. He had ranged more widely across Earth's surface as well as through Earth's duration than was feasible for subordinates, transport being as limited as it was. He had conducted interviews and interrogations, which others must not lest too many events of that sort arouse somebody's suspicions.

He knew the Eyrie would be here, under his control, for the next two centuries. He had met himself then, who told him how satisfactorily Phase One of the plan had been carried out. At that date, the vastly augmented force he was shown must evacuate this stronghold. Nuclei of renascent civilization were spreading across all America, the Maurai were everywhere, a realm like his could no longer stay isolated nor maintain the pretense its leaders were nothing extraordinary.

A new base had been (would be) constructed uptime. He visited it, and found it totally unlike the old. Here were modern materials, sleek construction—mostly underground—housing advanced machinery, automation, a thermonuclear powerplant.

This was in the era of revolt against the Maurai. They had in the end failed to convert to their philosophy the gigantically various whole of mankind. Doubts, discontents, rebelliousness among their own people led to vacillation in foreign policy. One defiant nation redeveloped the fusion energy generator; and it made no attempt at secrecy. Old countries and alliances were disintegrating, new being born in turmoil.

"Always we need patience as well as boldness and briskness," Wallis wrote. "We will have far more resources than we do in Phase One, and far more skill in employing them. That includes the use of time travel to multiply the size of a military force, each man doubling back again and again till the opposition is overwhelmed. But I am well aware this sort of thing has its limits and hazards. In no case can we hope to take over the whole world quickly. An empire which is to last thousands of years is bound to be slow in the building."

Was that how Phase Two would end: with a planet once more pastoralized, in order that the overlordship of the Eyrie men, in the fabulous engines they would have developed, be unchallengable? Wallis believed it. He believed Phase Three would consist of the benign remolding of that society by its new masters, the creation of a wholly new kind of man. Ranging very far uptime, he had glimpsed marvels he could not begin to describe.

But he seemed vague in this part of his book. Exact information was maddeningly hard to gather. He meant to continue doing so, though more and more by proxy. In general, he recognized, his lifespan would be spent on Phase One. The self he met at its end was an aged man.

"Let us be satisfied to be God's agents of redemption," he wrote. "However, those who wish may cherish a private hope. Is it not possible that at last science will find a way to make the old young again, to make the body immortal? And by then, I have no doubt, time travel will be understood, may even be commonplace. Will not that wonderful future return and seek us out, who brought it into being, and give us our reward?"

Havig's mouth tightened. He thought: *I've seen what happens when you try to straitjacket man into an ideology.*

But later he thought: *There is a lot of flexibility here. We could conceivably end more as teachers than masters.*

And finally: *I'll stick around awhile, at least. The alternative to serving him seems to be to let my gift go for nothing, my life go down in futility.*

Krasicki summoned him. It was a steely-cold day. Sunlight shattered into brilliance on icicles hanging from turrets. Havig shivered as he crossed the courtyard to the office.

Uniformed, Krasicki sat in a room as neat and functional as a cell. "Be seated," he ordered. The chair was hard, and squeaked.

"Do you judge yourself ready for your work?" he asked.

A thrill went through Havig. His pulses hammered. "Y-yes. Anxious to start. I—" He straightened. "Yes."

Krasicki shuffled some papers on his desk. "I have been watching your progress," he said, "and considering how we might best employ you. That includes minimum risk to yourself. You have had a good deal of extratemporal experience on your own, I know, which makes you already valuable. But you've not hitherto been on a mission for us." He offered a stiff little smile. "The idea which came to me springs from your special background."

Havig somehow maintained a cool exterior.

"We must expand our capabilities, particularly recruiting," Krasicki said. "Well, you've declared yourself reasonably fluent in the Greek *koinê*. You've described a visit you made to Byzantine Constantinople. That seems like a strategic place from which to begin a systematic search through the medieval period."

"Brilliant!" Havig cried, suddenly happy and excited. It rushed from him: "Center of civilization, everything flowed through the Golden Horn, and, and what we could do as traders—"

Krasicki lifted a palm. "Hold. Perhaps later, when we have more manpower, a wider network, perhaps then that will be worthwhile. But at present we're too sharply limited in the man-years available to us. We cannot squander them. Never forget, we must complete Phase One by a definite date. No, Havig, what is necessary is a quicker and more direct approach."

"What—?"

"Given a large hoard of coin and treasure, we can finance ourselves in an era when this is currency. But you know yourself how cumbersome is the transportation of goods through time. Therefore we must acquire our capital on . . . on the spot? . . . yes, on the spot. And, as I said, quickly."

Havig's suspicions exploded in dismay. "You can't mean by robbery!"

"No, no, no." Krasicki shook his head. "Think. Listen. A raid on a peaceful city, massive enough to reap a useful harvest, that would be dangerously conspicuous. Could get into the history books, and that could wreck our cover. Besides, it would be dangerous in itself, too. Our men would have small numbers, not overly well supplied with firearms. They would not have powered vehicles. The Byzantine army and police were usually large and well-disciplined. No, I don't propose madness."

"What, then?"

"Taking advantage of chaos, in order to remove what would otherwise be stolen by merciless invaders for no good purpose."

Havig stared.

"In 1204," his superior went on, "Constantinople was captured by the armies of the Fourth Crusade. They plundered it from end to end; what remained was a broken shell." He waved an arm. "Why should we not take a share? It's lost to the owners anyway." He peered at the other's face before adding: "And, to be sure, we arrange compensation, give them protection from slaughter and rapine, help them rebuild their lives."

"Judas priest!" Havig choked. "A hijacking!"

Having briefed himself in the Eyrie's large microtape library, having had a costume made and similar details taken care of, he embarked.

An aircraft deposited him near the twenty-first-century ruins of Istanbul and took off again into the air as quickly as he into the past. A lot of radioactivity lingered in these ashes. He hadn't yet revealed the fact of his chronolog and must find his target by the tedious process of counting sun-traverses, adding an estimate of days missed, making an initial emergence, and zeroing in by trial and error.

Leonce had been furious at being left behind. But she lacked the knowledge to be useful here, except as companion and consoler. Indeed, she would have been a liability, her extreme foreignness drawing stares. Havig meant to pass for a Scandinavian on pilgrimage—Catholic, true, but less to be detested than a Frenchman, Venetian, Aragonese, anyone from those western Mediterranean nations which pressed wolfishly in on the dying Empire. As a Russian he would have been more welcome. But Russians were common thereabouts, and their Orthodox faith made them well understood. He dared not risk a slip.

He didn't start in the year of the conquest. That would be too turbulent, and every outsider too suspect, for the detailed study he must make. The Crusaders actually entered Constantinople in 1203, after a naval siege, to install a puppet on its throne. They hung around to collect their pay before proceeding to the Holy Land. The puppet found his coffers empty, and temporized. Friction between East Romans and "Franks" swelled to terrifying proportions. In January 1204, Alexius, son-in-law of the deposed Emperor, got together sufficient force to seize palace and crown. For three months he and his people strove to drive the Crusaders off. Their hope that God would somehow come to their aid collapsed when Alexius, less gallant than they, despaired and fled. The Crusaders marched back through opened portals. They had worked themselves into homicidal self-righteousness about "Greek perfidy," and the horror began almost at once.

Havig chose spring, because it was a beautiful season, in 1195, because that was amply far downtime, for his basic job of survey. He carried well-forged documents which got him past the city guards, and gold pieces to exchange for *nomismae*. After finding a room in a good inn—nothing like the pigsty he'd have had to endure in the West—he started exploring.

His prior visit had been to halcyon 1050. The magnificence he now encountered, the liveliness and cosmopolitan colorfulness, were no less. However raddled her dominion, New Rome remained the queen of Europe.

Havig saw her under the shadow.

* * *

The house and shop of Doukas Manasses, goldsmith, stood on a hill near the middle of the city. Square-built neighbors elbowed it, all turning blind faces onto the steep, wide, well-paved and well-swept street. But from its flat roof you had a superb view, from end to end of the vast, towered walls which enclosed the city, and further: across a maze of thoroughfares, a countlessness of dwellings and soaring church domes; along the grand avenue called the Mesê to flowering countryside past the Gate of Charisius, on inward by columns which upbore statuary from the noblest days of Hellas, monasteries and museums and libraries which preserved works by men like Aeschylus and women like Sappho that later centuries would never read, through broad forums pulsing with life, to the Hippodrome and that sprawling splendid complex which was the Imperial Palace. On a transverse axis, vision reached from glittering blue across the Sea of Marmora to a mast-crowded Golden Horn and the rich suburbs and smaragdine heights beyond.

Traffic rivered. The noise of wheels, hoofs, feet, talk, song, laughter, sobbing, cursing, praying, blended together into one ceaseless heartbeat. A breeze carried a richness of odors, sea, woodsmoke, food, animals, humanity. Havig breathed deep.

"Thank you, Kyrios Hauk," Doukas Manasses said. "You are most courteous to praise this sight." His manner implied mild surprise that a Frank would not sneer at everything Greek. To be sure, Hauk Thomasson was not really a Frank or one of the allied English, he was from a boreal kingdom.

"Less courteous than you, Kyrios Manasses, to show me it," Havig replied.

They exchanged bows. The Byzantines were not basically a strict folk—besides their passionate religion and passionate sense for beauty, they had as much bustling get-up-and-go, as much inborn gusto, as Levantines in any era—but their upper classes set store by ceremonious politeness.

"You expressed interest," Doukas said. He was a gray-bearded man with handsome features and nearsighted eyes. His slight frame seemed lost in the usual dalmatic robe.

"I merely remarked, Kyrios, that a shop which produced such elegance as does yours must be surrounded by inspiration." You could case public buildings easily enough; but your way to learn what private hands held what wealth was to go in, say you were looking for a gift to take home, and inspect a variety of samples.

Well, dammit, Doukas and his apprentices did do exquisite work.

"You are too kind," the goldsmith murmured. "Although I do feel—since all good stems from God—that we Romans should look more to His creation, less to conventionality, than we have done."

"Like this?" Having pointed at a blossoming crabapple tree in a larger planter.

Doukas smiled. "That's for my daughter. She loves flowers, and we cannot take her daily on an outing in the country."

Women enjoyed an honorable status, with many legal rights and protections. But perhaps Doukas felt his visitor needed further explanation: "We may indulge her too much, my Anna and I. However, she's our only. That is, I was wedded before, but the sons of sainted Eudoxia are grown. Xenia is Anna's first, and my first daughter."

On impulse he added: "Kyrios Hauk, think me not overbold. But I'm fascinated to meet a . . . friendly . . . foreigner, from so remote a country at that. It is long since there were many from your lands in the Varangian Guard.

I would enjoy conversing at leisure. Would you honor our home at the evening meal?"

"Why—why, thank you." Havig thought what a rare chance this was to find things out. Byzantine trades and crafts were organized in tight guilds under the direction of the prefect. This man, being distinguished in his profession, probably knew all about his colleagues, and a lot about other businesses, "I should be delighted."

"Would you mind, my guest, if wife and child share our board?" Doukas asked shyly. "They will not interrupt. Yet they'd be glad to hear you. Xenia is, well, forgive my pride, she's only five and already learning to read."

She was a singularly beautiful child.

Hauk Thomasson returned next year and described the position he had accepted with a firm in Athens. Greece belonged to the Empire, and would till the catastrophe; but so much trade was now under foreign control that the story passed. His work would often bring him to Constantinople. He was happy to have this opportunity of renewing acquaintanceship, and hoped the daughter of Kyrios Manasses would accept a small present—

"Athens!" the goldsmith whispered. "You dwell in the soul of Hellas?" He reached up to lay both hands on his visitor's shoulders. Tears stood in his eyes. "Oh, wonderful for you, wonderful! To see those temples is the dream of my life . . . God better me, more than to see the Holy Land."

Xenia accepted the toy gratefully. At dinner and afterward she listened, rapt, till her nanny shooed her to bed. She was a sweet youngster, Havig thought, undeniably bright, and not spoiled even though it seemed Anna would bear no more children.

He enjoyed himself, too. A cultured, sensitive, observant man is a pleasure to be with in any age. This assignment was, for a while, losing its nightmare quality.

In truth, he simply skipped ahead through time. He must check up periodically, to be sure events didn't make his original data obsolete. Simultaneously he could develop more leads, ask more questions, than would have been practical in a single session.

But—he wondered a few calendar years later—wasn't he being more thorough than needful? Did he really have to make this many visits to the Manasses family, become an intimate, join them on holidays and picnics, invite them out to dinner or for a day on a rented pleasure barge? Certainly he was exceeding his expense estimate. . . . To hell with that. He could finance himself by placing foreknowledgeable bets on events in the Hippodrome. An agent working alone had broad discretion.

He felt guilty about lying to his friends. But it had to be. After all, his objective was to save them.

Xenia's voice was somewhat high and thin, but whenever he heard or remembered it, Havig would think of songbirds. Thus had it been since first she overcame her timidity and laughed in his presence. From then on, she chattered with him on the limit her parents allowed, or more when they weren't looking.

She was reed-slender. He had never seen any human who moved with more gracefulness; and when decorum was not required, her feet danced. Her hair was a midnight mass which, piled on her head, seemed as if it ought to bend the delicate neck. Her skin was pale and clear; her face was oval, tilt-nosed, its lips always a little parted. The eyes dominated that countenance, enormous, heavy-lashed, luminous black. Those eyes may be seen elsewhere, in a Ravenna mosaic, upon Empress Theodora the Great; they may never be forgotten.

It was a strange thing to meet her at intervals of months which for Havig were hours or days. Each time, she was so dizzyingly grown. In awe he felt a sense of that measureless river which he could swim but on which she could only be carried from darkness to darkness.

The house was built around a courtyard where flowers and oranges grew and a fountain played. Doukas proudly showed Havig his latest acquisition: on a pedestal in one corner, a bust of Constantine who made Rome Christian and for whom New Rome was named. "From the life, I feel sure," he said. "By then the art of portrayal was losing its former mastery. Nevertheless, observe his imperiously tight-held mouth—"

Nine-year-old Xenia giggled. "What is it, dear?" her father asked.

"Nothing, really," she said, but couldn't stop giggling.

"No, do tell us. I shan't be angry."

"He . . . he . . . he wants to make a very important speech, and he has gas!"

"By Bacchus," Havig exclaimed, "she's right!"

Doukas struggled a moment before he gave up and joined the fun.

"Oh, please, will you not come to church with us, Hauk?" she begged. "You don't know how lovely it is, when the song and incense and candleflames rise up to Christ Pantocrator." She was eleven and overflowing with God.

"I'm sorry," Havig said. "You know I am, am Catholic."

"The saints won't mind. I asked Father and Mother, and they won't mind either. We can say you're a Russian, if we need to. I'll show you how to act." She tugged his hand. "Do come!"

He yielded, not sure whether she hoped to convert him

or merely wanted to share something glorious with her honorary uncle.

"But it's too wonderful!" She burst into tears and hugged her thirteenth birthday present to her before holding it out. "Father, Mother, see what Hauk gave me! This book, the p-p-plays of Euripides—all of them—for *me*!"

When she was gone to change clothes for a modest festival dinner, Doukas said: "That was a royal gift. Not only the cost of having the copy made and binding it as a codex. The thought."

"I knew she loves the ancients as much as you do," the traveler answered.

"Forgive me," Anna the mother said. "But at her age . . . may Euripides not be, well, stern reading?"

"These are stern times," Havig replied, and could no longer feign joy. "A tragic line may hearten her to meet fate." He turned to the goldsmith. "Doukas, I tell you again, I swear to you, I know through my connections that the Venetians at this very moment are negotiating with other Frankish lords—"

"You have said that." The goldsmith nodded. His hair and beard were nearly white.

"It's not too late to move you and your family to safety. I'll help."

"Where is safety better than these walls, which no invader has ever breached? Or where, if I break up my shop, where is safety from pauperdom and hunger? What would my apprentices and servants do? They can't move. No, my good old friend, prudence and duty alike tells us we must remain here and trust in God." Doukas uttered a small sad chuckle. " 'Old,' did I say? You never seem to change. Well, you're in your prime, of course."

Havig swallowed. "I don't think I'll be back in Constantinople for some while. My employers, under present circumstances— Be careful. Keep unnoticeable, hide your wealth, stay off the streets whenever you can and always at night. I know the Franks."

"Well, I, I'll bear your advice in mind, Hauk, if— But you go too far. This is New Rome."

Anna touched the arms of both. Her smile was uncertain. "Now that's enough politics, you men," she said. "Take off those long faces. We're making merry on Xenia's day. Have you forgotten?"

Time-skipping in an alley across the street, Havig checked the period of the first Latin occupation. Nothing terrible seemed to happen. The house drew back into itself and waited.

He went pastward to a happier year, took a night's lodging, forced himself to eat a hearty supper and get a lot of sleep. Next morning he omitted breakfast: a good idea when you may soon be in combat.

He jumped ahead, to the twelfth of April, 1204.

He could be no more than an observer through the days and nights of the sack. His orders were explicit and made sense: "If you can possibly avoid it, stay out of danger. Under no conditions mingle, or try to influence events. Absolutely never, and this is under penalties, never enter a building which is a scene of action. We want your report, and for that we need you alive."

Fire leaped and roared. Smoke drifted bitter. People huddled like rats indoors, or fled like rats outside, and some escaped but thousands were ridden down, shot down, chopped down, beaten, stomped, tortured, robbed, raped, by yelling sooty sweaty blood-splattered men whose fleas hopped about on silks and altar cloths they had flung across their shoulders. Corpses gaped in the gutters, which ran red till they clotted. Many of the bodies were very small. Mothers crept about shrieking for children, children for mothers; most fathers lay dead. Orthodox priests in their churches were kept in pain until they revealed where the treasury was hidden; usually there was none, in which case it was great sport to soak their beards in oil and set these alight. Women, girls, nuns of any age lay mumbling or whimpering after a row of men had violated them. Humiliations more ingenious might be contrived.

A drunken harlot sat on the patriach's throne in Hagia Sophia, while dice games for plunder were played on the altars. The bronze horses of the Hippodrome were carted off to Venice's Cathedral of St. Mark; artwork, jewelry, sacred objects would be scattered across a continent; but at least these things were preserved. More was melted down or torn apart for the precious metals and stones, or smashed or burned for amusement. So perished much classical art, and nearly all classical writing, which Constantinople had kept safe until these days. It was not true that the Turks of 1453 were responsible. The Crusaders were there before them.

Afterward came the great silence, broken by furtive crying, and the stench, and the sickness, and the hunger.

In this wise, at the beginning of that thirteenth century which Catholic apologists call the apogee of civilization, did Western Christendom destroy its Eastern flank. A century and a half later, having devoured Asia Minor, the Turks entered Europe.

Havig time-skipped.

He would return to a safe date, seek out one of his chosen sites, and advance through the whole period of the sack, flickering in and out of normal time, until he knew what was to happen there. When he saw a Frankish band enter a place, he focused more sharply. In most cases they staggered out after a while, sated with death and torment, kicking prisoners who carried away their spoils. Those buildings he wrote off. You couldn't change the past or future, you could merely discover what parts were your own.

But in certain instances—and only a comparative few would be accessible to the Eyrie commandos; they hadn't many man-months to spend on this job—

Havig saw marauders frightened off, or cut down if need be, by submachine-gun fire. The spectacle did not make him gloat. However, he knew a chilly satisfaction while he recorded the spot.

From it, the Eyrie men would cart their loot. They were dressed in conqueror style. Amidst this confusion, it was unlikely they would attract notice. A ship was arranged for, to bear the gains to a safe depot.

They would take care of the dwellers, Krasicki had promised. What to do would depend on circumstances. Some families need simply be left unharmed, with enough money to carry on. Others must be guided elsewhere and staked to a fresh beginning.

Paradoxes need not be feared. The tale of how veritable saints—or demons, if one was a Frank—had rescued so-and-so might live a while in folklore but would not get into any chronicle. Writers in Constantinople must be cautious for the next fifty-seven years, until Michael Paleologus ended the Latin kingdom and raised a ghost of Empire. By then, anecdotes would have been lost.

Havig didn't look into the immediate sequels of these agent actions. Besides the prohibition laid on him, he already was overburdened. Many sights he witnessed sent him fleeing downtime, weeping and vomiting, to sleep till he had the strength to continue.

The Manasses home was among the earliest he investigated. It wasn't quite the first; he wanted to gain experience elsewhere; but he knew he was going to be dulled later on.

He had cherished a hope it might be entirely overlooked. Some of his points were. It being unfeasible to check the Crusaders in the famous places, he had investigated lesser ones, whose aggregate wealth was what counted. And Constantinople was too big, too labyrinthine, too rich and strange for the pillagers to break down every door.

He felt no extreme fears. In this particular case, *something* would be done if need be, by himself if nobody else, and Caleb Wallis could take his destiny and stuff it. Nevertheless, when Havig from his alley saw a dozen filthy men lope toward that open entrance, the heart stumbled within him. When lead sleeted from it, and three Franks fell and were quiet, two lay sprattling and shrieking, and the rest howled and fled, Havig cheered.

His return was a sizable operation in itself.

Between the radioactivity and the time uncertainty, he couldn't proceed up to dead Istanbul and hunt around for an agreed-on hour at which the aircraft would meet him. Nor could he appear in an earlier epoch—the Eyrie's planes were not available then—or at a later one—the site would be reoccupied. He'd look too peculiar, and would still have the problem of reaching a geographical point where contact could be made.

"Now you tell me!" he muttered to himself. For a while he marveled that the obvious answer hadn't occurred when this whole project was being discussed. Use his twentieth-century *persona*. Cache some funds and clothes in a contemporary Istanbul hotel; feed the management a line about being involved in production of a movie; and there he was, set.

Well, he'd been overwhelmed by things to think about. And the idea hadn't come to anyone else. While Wallis employed some gadgets developed in the High Years, he and his lieutenants were nineteenth-century men who had organized an essentially nineteenth-century operation.

The plan called for Havig to double back downtime, make more money if he had to, engage passage on a ship to Crete, there find a specific isolated spot, and project himself uptime.

Actually, effort, cramped quarters, dirt, noise, smells, moldy hardtack, scummy water, weird fellow passengers, and all, he didn't care. He needed something to take his mind off what he had seen.

"Splendidly done," Krasicki said across the written report. "Splendidly, I'm sure the Sachem will give you public praise and reward, when next your two time-lines intersect."

"Hm? Oh. Oh, yeah. Thanks." Havig blinked.

Krasicki studied him. "You are exhausted, are you not?"

"Call me Rip van Winkle," Havig muttered.

Krasicki understood his gauntness, sunken eyes, slumped body, tic in cheek, if not the reference. "Yes. It is common. We allow for it. You have earned a furlough. In your home milieu, I suggest. Never mind about the rest of the Constantinople business. If we need more from you, we can always ask when you return here." His smile approached warmth. "Go, now. We'll talk later. I think we can arrange for your girl friend to accompany—Havig? Havig?"

Havig was asleep.

His trouble was that later, instead of enjoying his leave, he started thinking.

chapter 10

He woke with his resolve crystallized. It was early. Light over the high rooftops of the Rive Gauche, Paris, 1965, reached gray and as cool as the air, which traffic had not yet begun to trouble. The hotel room was shadowy. Leonce breathed warm and tousle-haired beside him. They had been night-clubbing late—among the *chansonniers*, which he preferred, now that her wish for the big glittery shows was slaked—and come back to make leisured and tender love. She'd hardly stir before a knock, some hours hence, announced coffee and croissants.

Havig was surprised at his own rousing. Well, more and more in the past couple of weeks, he'd felt he was only postponing the inevitable. His conscience must have gotten tired of nagging him and delivered an ultimatum.

Regardless of danger, he felt at peace, for the first time in that whole while.

He rose, washed and dressed, assembled his gear. It lay ready, two modules within his baggage. There was the basic agent's kit, an elaborated version of what he had taken to Jerusalem plus a gun. (The Eyrie's documents section furnished papers to get that past customs.) He had omitted items Leonce had in hers, such as most of the silver, in order to save the mass of the chronolog. (He had unobtrusively taken it back with him on this trip. She asked him why he lugged it around. When he said, "Special electronic gear," the incantation satisfied her.) Passport, vaccination certificate, and thick wallet of traveler's checks completed the list.

For a minute he stood above the girl. She was a dear, he thought. Her joy throughout their tour had been a joy to him. Dirty trick, sneaking out on her. Should he leave a note? . . . No, no reason for it. He **could** return to this hour. If he didn't, well, she knew enough contemporary English and procedure, and had enough funds, to handle the rest. (Her own American passport was genuine; the Eyrie had made her a birth certificate.) She might perhaps feel hurt if she knew what had gotten him killed.

Chances were he was simply courting a reprimand. In that case, she'd hear the full story; but he'd be there to explain, in terms of loyalty which she could understand.

Or would it much matter? That she called him "darlya" and spoke of love when he embraced her was probably just her way. Lately, though, she'd been holding his hand a lot when they were out together, and he'd caught her smiling at him when she thought he wasn't noticing. . . . He was a bit in love with her too. It could never last, but while it did—

He stooped. "So long, Big Red," he whispered. His lips brushed hers. Straightening, he picked up his two carrying cases and stole from the room. By evening he was in Istanbul.

The trip took this many hours out of his lifespan, mostly spent on the plane and airport buses. Time-hopping around among ticket agencies and the like made the calendrical interval a couple of days. He had told me through a wry grin: "Know where the best place usually is for unnoticed chronokinesis in a modern city? Not Superman's telephone booth. A public lavatory stall. Real romantic, huh?"

He ate a good though lonely dinner, and in his luxurious though lonely chamber took a sleeping pill. He needed to be rested before he embarked.

Constantinople, late afternoon on the thirteenth of April, 1204. Havig emerged in an alley downhill from his destination. Silence pressed upon him—no slap of buskins, clop of hoofs, rumble and squeal of cartwheels, no song of bells, no voices talking, chaffering, laughing, dreaming aloud, no children at their immemorial small games. But the stillness had background, a distant jagged roar which was fire and human shrieking, the nearer desperate bark of a dog.

He made ready. The gun, a 9-mm. Smith & Wesson mule-killer, he holstered at his waist. Extra ammunition he put in the deep pockets of his jacket. Kit and chronolog he strapped together in an aluminum packframe which went on his back.

Entering the street, he saw closed doors, shuttered windows. Most dwellers were huddled inside, hungry, thirsty, endlessly at prayer. The average place wasn't worth breaking into, except for the pleasures of rape, murder, torture, and arson. True, this was the district of the goldsmiths. But not every building, or even a majority, belonged to one. Residential sections were not based on economic status; the poor could be anywhere. With booths and other displays removed, you couldn't tell if a particular façade concealed wealth or a tenement house—

—until, of course, you clapped hands on a local person and wrenched the information out of him.

Evidently those who rushed the Manasses home were in advance of the mobs which would surely boil hither as soon as palace and church buildings were stripped. Were they here yet? Havig hadn't been sure of the exact time when he saw them.

He trotted around a corner. A man lay dead of a stab wound. His right arm reached across his back, pulled from its socket. A shabby-clad woman crouched above him. As Havig passed, she screamed: "Wasn't it enough that you made him betray our neighbor? In Christ's name, wasn't that enough?"

No, he thought. There was also the peculiar thrill in extinguishing a life.

He went on by. The agony he had seen earlier returned to him in so monstrous a flood that the tears of this widow were lost. He could do nothing for her; trousers, short hair, shaven chin marked him a Frank in her eyes. When he was born, she and her grief were seven hundred years forgotten.

At least, he thought, he knew how the Crusaders had located Doukas's shop. One among them must understand some Greek, and their band had decided to seek out this part of town ahead of the rush. He knew also that his scheduling was approximately right.

Yells, clangor, and a terrible stammer reverberated wall to wall, off the cobbles, up to soot-befouled heaven. He stretched lips over teeth. "Yeah," he muttered, "I got it *exactly* right."

He quickened his pace. His younger self would be gone by the time he arrived. Obvious: he had not seen his later self. He didn't want that house unwatched for many minutes.

Not after considering what sort of man the average Eyrie warrior was.

The street of his goal was steep. Gravity dragged at him. He threw his muscles against it. His bootsoles thudded like his heart. His mouth was dry. Smoke stung his nostrils.

There!

One of the wounded Crusaders saw him, struggled to his knees, raised arms. Blood shone its wild red, hiding the cross on the surcoat, dripping in thick gouts to the stones. "*Ami,*" croaked from a face contorted out of shape, on whose waxenness the beard stubble stood blue. "*Frère par Iesu*—" The other survivor could merely groan, over and over.

Havig felt an impulse to kick their teeth in, and immediate shame. Mortal combat corrupts, and war corrupts absolutely. He ignored the kneeling man, who slumped behind him; he lifted both hands and shouted in English:

"Hold your fire! I am from the Eyrie! Inspection! Hold your fire and let me in!" Not without a tightness in his own unriddled guts, he approached the doorway.

An oxcart stood by, the animal tethered to a bracket which had formerly upheld Doukas's sign, twitching its ears against flies and with mild interest watching the Crusaders die. It would have been arranged for beforehand, to bring gold and silver and precious stones, ikons and ornaments and bridal chaplets, down to the ship which waited. Havig wasn't the only traveler who had been busy in the years before today. An operation like this took a great deal of work.

Nobody guarded the entrance. Armed as they were, the agents could deal with interference, not that any such attempt would be made. Havig stopped. Scowling, he examined the door. It was massive, and had surely been barred. The Franks had doubtless meant to chop their way in. But at the point when Havig glimpsed them and halted for a clear look, it had stood open. That was one fact which had never stopped plaguing him.

From the way it sagged on its hinges, scorched and half

splintered, Wallis's boys must have used a dynamite charge. That had been done so quickly that, in Havig's dim chronokinetic sight, their arrival had blurred together with that of the Franks a few minutes afterward.

Why had they forced an entrance? Such impatience would panic the household, complicate the task of assisting it to safety.

A scream fled down the rooms inside: *"No, oh, no, please!"* in Greek and Xenia's voice, followed by an oath and a guffaw. Havig crouched back as if stabbed.

In spite of everything, he had come late. At the moment of his arrival, the agents had already blown down the door and entered. They'd posted a man here to await the plunderers whom Havig had reported. Now he'd gone back within to join the fun.

For an instant which had no end, Havig cursed his own stupidity. Or naïveté—he was new to this kind of thing, bound to overlook essentials. To hell with that. Here he was and now he was, and his duty was to save whatever might be left.

His call must not have been noticed. He repeated it while he went through the remembered house. That sobbed-out cry for mercy had come from the largest chamber, which was the main workshop and storeroom.

Family, apprentices, and servants had been brought together there. It was more light and airy than usual in Byzantium, for a door and broad windows opened on the patio. Yonder the fountain still tinkled and twinkled, oranges glowed amid dark-green leaves, Eastertide flowerbeds were budding, the bust of Constantine stood in eternal embarrassment. Here, on shelves and tables, everywhere crowded that beauty which Doukas Manasses had seen to the making of.

He sprawled near the entrance. His skull was split open. The blood had spread far, making the floor slippery, staining footwear which then left crimson tracks. But much had soaked into his robe and white beard. One hand still held a tiny anvil, with which he must have tried to defend his women.

Four agents were present, dressed as Crusaders. In a flash, Havig knew them. Mendoza, of the Tijuana underworld in his own century, who had been among those who went to Jerusalem, was in charge. He was ordering the natives to start collecting loot. Moriarty, nineteenth-century Brooklyn gangster, kept guard, submachine gun at the ready. Hans, sixteenth-century *Landsknecht*, watched Coenraad of Brabant, who had wanted to draw sword and save the Savior, struggle with Xenia.

The girl screamed and screamed. She was only fourteen. Her hair had fallen loose. Sweat and tears plastered locks to her face. Coenraad grasped her around the waist. His free hand ripped at her gown. A war hammer, stuck in his belt, dripped blood and brains.

"Me next," Hans grinned. "Me next."

Coenraad bore Xenia down to the wet floor and fumbled with his trousers. Anna, who had stood as if blind and deaf near the body of her husband, wailed. She scuttled toward her daughter. Hans decked her with a single blow. "Maybe you later," he said.

"Hard men, you two," Moriarty laughed. "Real hard, hey?"

The sequence had taken seconds. Havig's call had again failed to pierce their excitement. Mendoza was first to see him, and exclaim. The rest froze, until Coenraad let Xenia go and climbed to his feet.

She stared up. Never had he thought to see such a light as was born in her eyes. "Hauk!" she cried. "Oh, Hauk!"

Mendoza swung his gun around. "What is this?" he demanded.

Havig realized how far his own hand was from his own

weapon. But he felt no fear—hardly any emotion, in fact, on the surface, beyond a cougar alertness. Down underneath roiled the fury, sorrow, horror, disgust he could not now afford.

"I might ask you the same," he replied slowly.

"Have you forgotten your orders? I know them. Your job is to gather intelligence. You are not to risk yourself at a scene of operations like this."

"I finished my job, Mendoza. I came back for a personal look."

"Forbidden! Get out, and we'll talk later about whether or not I report you."

"Suppose I don't?" Despite control, Havig heard his voice rise, high and saw-edged: "I've seen what I wasn't supposed to see in one lump, only piece by piece, gradually, so I'd make the dirty little compromises till it no longer mattered, I'd be in so deep that I'd either have to kill myself or become like you. Yes, I understand."

Mendoza's shrug did not move the tommygun barrel aimed at Havig's stomach. "Well? What do you expect? We use what human material we can find. These boys are no worse than the Crusaders—than man in most of history. Are they, Jack? Be honest."

"They are. Because they have the power to come into any time, any place, do anything, and never fear revenge. How do they spend their holidays, I wonder? I imagine the taste for giving pain and death must grow with practice."

"Listen—"

"And Wallis, his whole damned outfit, doesn't even try to control them!"

"Havig, you talk too much. Get out before I arrest you."

"They keep the few like me from knowing, till we've accepted that crock—about how the mission of the Eyrie is too important for us to waste lifespan on enforcing common humanity. Right?"

Mendoza spat. "Hokay, boy, you said plenty and then some. You're under arrest. You'll be escorted uptime and the Sachem will judge your case. Be good and maybe you'll get off easy."

For a moment it was tableau, very quiet save for Xenia's sobs where she cradled the head of her half-conscious mother. Her eyes never left Havig. Nor did those of the household he had known—hopeful young Bardas, gifted Ioannes, old Maria who had been Xenia's nurse, all and all of the dozen—nor those of Mendoza and Moriarty. Hans's kept flickering in animal wariness, Coenraad's in thwarted lechery.

Havig reached his decision, made his plan, noted the position of each man and weapon, in that single hard-held breath.

Himself appeared, sixfold throughout the room. The firefight exploded.

He cast himself back in time a few minutes while sidestepping, sped uptime while he drew his pistol, emerged by Hans. The gun cracked and kicked. The *Landsknecht*'s head geysered into pieces. Havig went back again, and across the chamber.

Afterward he scarcely remembered what happened. The battle was too short, too ferocious. Others could do what he did, against him. Coenraad wasn't quick-witted enough, and died. Moriarty vanished from Havig's sight as the latter arrived. Mendoza's gun blasted, and Havig sprang futureward barely in time. Traveling, he saw Moriarty's shadow form appear. He backtracked, was there at the instant, shot the man and twisted off into time, away from Mendoza.

Then the Mexican wasn't present. Havig slipped pastward—a night when the family slept at peace under God—to gasp air and let the sweat stop spurting, the limbs stop shaking. At last he felt able to return and scan the period of combat in detail. Beyond a certain point, not long after the beginning, he found no Mendoza.

The fellow must have gone way uptime, maybe to the far side of the Judgment, for help.

This meant fast action was vital. Havig's friends could not time-hop. The enemy would be, no, were handicapped by the difficulty of reaching a precise goal without a chronolog. But they could cast around, and wouldn't miss by much.

Havig rejoined Earth at the earliest possible second. Moriarty threshed about, yammering anguish, like those men outside whom he, perhaps, had been the one to shoot. Never mind him. The Byzantines huddled together. Bardas lay dead, two others wounded in crossfire.

"I come to save you," Havig said into the reek of powder and fear, into their uncomprehending glazed-eye shock. He drew the sign of the cross, right to left in Orthodox style. "In the name of the Father, and of the Son, and of the Holy Ghost. In the name of the Virgin Mary and every saint. Come with me, at once, or you die."

He helped Xenia rise. She clung to him, face buried against his breast, fingers clutching. He rumpled the long black hair and remembered how he a child would grasp at a father bound for death. Across her shoulder he snapped: "Ioannes, Nicephorus, you look in the best shape. Carry your lady Anna. The rest of you who're hale, give aid to the hurt." English broke from him: "Goddammit, we've got to get out of here!"

Numbly, they obeyed. In the street he stopped to don the surcoat off a dead Crusader. His pack he gave a man to carry. From another corpse he took a sword. He didn't waste time unbuckling the scabbard belt. That weapon indicated a high enough rank that his party wasn't likely to meet interference.

Several streets down, dizziness overwhelmed him. He must sit, head between knees, till strength returned. Xenia knelt before him, hands anxiously trying to help. "Hauk," went her raw whisper. "Wh-wh-what's wrong, dearest Hauk?"

"We're safe," he finally said.

From the immediate threat, at least. He didn't suppose the Eyrie would spend man-years scouring Constantinople for him and these, once they had vanished into the multitudes. But he had still to safeguard their tomorrows, and his own. The knowledge gave him a glacial kind of resolution. He rose and led them further on their stumbling way.

"I left them at a certain monastery," he told me (long afterward on his own world line). "The place was jammed with refugees, but I foreknew it'd escape attention. In the course of the next several days, local time, I made better arrangements. A simple task—" he grimaced—"distasteful but simple, to hijack unidentifiable loot from ordinary Franks. I made presents to that monastery, and to the nunnery where I later took the women. This won favor for the people I'd brought, special favor out of the hordes, because with my donations the monks and nuns could buy bread to feed their poor."

"What about the hordes?" I asked softly.

He covered his face. "What could I do? They were too many."

I gripped his shoulder. "They are always too many, Jack."

He sighed and smiled a little. "Thanks, Doc."

I had exceeded my day's tobacco ration, but the hour was far into night and my nerves required some help. Drawing out my pipe, I made an evil-smelling ceremony of cleaning it. "What'd you do next?"

"Went back to the twentieth century—a different hotel—and slept a lot," he said. "Afterward . . . well, as for my Byzantines, I could do nothing in their immediate futures. I'd cautioned them against talking, told them to say they'd just fled from a raid. After a 'saint' had rescued them from 'demons,' it was a safe bet they'd obey. But as fail-safe, I did not tell the men where I led the women.

"Further than that, no transportation being available, and me not wanting to do anything which might make them noticeable, my best tactic was to leave them alone. The organized institutions where they were could care for them better than I'd know how.

"Besides, I had to provide for my own survival."

I reamed the pipe with needless force. "Yes, indeed," I said. "What did you do?"

He sipped his drink. While he dared not blur mind or senses, the occasional taste of Scotch was soothing. "I knew the last date on which I had publicly been J. F. Havig," he told me. "At the start of my furlough, in 1965, in conference with a broker of mine. True, there had been later appearances in normal time, like my 1969 trip to Israel, but those were brief. Nineteen sixty-five marked the end of what real continuity there was in my official *persona*. Everything was in order, the broker told me. I didn't see how so complicated a financial and identity setup could be faked. Thus my existence was safe up to that point."

"The Eyrie couldn't strike at you earlier? Why not?"

"Oh, they could appear at a previous moment and lay a trap of some kind, no doubt. But it couldn't be sprung till later. On the whole, I doubted they'd even try that. None of them really know their way around the twentieth century, its upper echelons in particular, as I do."

"You mean, an event once recorded is unalterable?"

Now his smile chilled me. "I suspect all events are," he said. "I do know a traveler cannot generate contradictions. I've tried. So have others, including Wallis himself. Let me give you a single, personal example. Once in young manhood I thought I'd go back downtime, break my 'uncle's' prohibition, reveal to my father what I was and warn him against enlisting."

"And?" I breathed.

"Doc, remember that broken leg of mine you treated?"

"Yes. Wait! That was—"

"Uh-huh. I tripped on an electric cord somebody had carelessly left at the top of some stairs, the personal-time day before I planned to set out. . . . When I was well and ready to start afresh, I got an urgent call from my trust company and had to argue over assorted tedious details. Returning to Senlac, I found my mother had made her final break with Birkelund and needed my presence. I looked at those two innocent babies he and she had brought into this world, and got the message."

"Does God intervene, do you think?"

"No, no, no. I suppose it's simply a logical impossibility to change the past, same as it's logically impossible for a uniformly colored spot to be both red and green. And every instant in time is the past of infinitely many other instants. That figures.

"The pattern *is*. Our occasional attempts to break it, and our failures, are part of *it*."

"Then we're nothing except puppets?"

"I didn't say that, Doc. In fact, I can't believe we are. Seems to me, our free wills must be a part of the grand design too. But we'd better take care to stay within the area of unknownness, which is where our freedom lies."

"Could this be analogous to, well, drugs?" I wondered. "A man might deliberately, freely take a chemical which grabbed hold of his mind. But then, while its effects lasted, he would not be free."

"Maybe, maybe." Havig stirred in his chair, peered out into night, took another small swallow of whiskey. "Look, we may not have time for these philosophical musings. Wallis's hounds are after me. If not in full cry, surely at any rate alert for any spoor of me. They know something of my biography. They can find out more, and make spot checks if nothing else."

"Is that why you avoided me, these past years of my life?" I asked.

"Yes." Now he laid a comforting hand on me. "While Kate lived—you understand?"

I nodded dumbly.

"What I did," he said, hastening on to dry detail, "was return to that selfsame date of 1965, in New York, the last one I could be reasonably sure of. From there I backtracked, laying a groundwork. It took a while. I had to make sure that what I did would be so hard to trace that Wallis wouldn't assign the necessary man-years to the task. I worked through Swiss banks, several series of dummies, et cetera. The upshot was that John Havig's fortune got widely distributed, in the names of a number of people and corporations who in effect are me. John Havig himself, publicity-shy playboy, explained to his hired financiers that this was because—never mind. A song and dance which sounded enough like a tax-fraud scheme, though actually it wasn't, that they were glad to wash their hands of me and to know nothing important.

"John Havig, you recall, thereupon quietly dropped out of circulation. Since he had no intimates in the twentieth century, apart from his mother and his old hometown doctor, only these would ever miss him or wonder much; and it was easy to drop them an occasional reassuring letter."

"Postcards to me, mainly," I said. "You had me wondering, all right." After a pause: "Where were you?"

"Having covered my tracks as well as might be," he answered, "I went back to Constantinople."

* * *

In the burnt-out husk of New Rome, order was presently restored. At first, if nothing else, troops needed water and food, for which labor and some kind of civil government were needed, which meant that the dwellers could no longer be harried like vermin. Later, Baldwin of Flanders, lord over that fragment of the Empire which became his portion and included the city, desired to get more use than that out of his subjects. He was soon captured in war against the Bulgarians and died a prisoner, but the attitude of his brother and successor Henry I was the same. A Latin king could oppress the Greeks, squeeze them, humiliate them, tax them to poverty, dragoon them into his corvées or his armies. But for this he must allow them a measure of security in their work and their lives.

Though Xenia was a guest, the nunnery was strict. She met Havig in a chilly brick-walled gloom, under the disapproving gaze of a sister. Robed in rough brown wool, coifed, veiled, she was forbidden to touch her male visitor, let alone seek his arms, no matter how generous a benefaction he had brought along. But he saw her Ravenna eyes; and the garments could not hide how she had begun to grow and fill out; nor could every tone in her voice be flattened, which brought back to him the birds on countryside days with her and her father—

"Oh, Hauk, darling Hauk!" Shrinking back, drawing the cross, starting to genuflect and hesitating a-tremble: "I . . . I beg your pardon, your forgiveness, B-b-blessed One."

The old nun frowned and took a step toward them. Havig waved wildly. "No, no, Xenia!" he exclaimed. "I'm as mortal as you are. I swear it. Strange things did happen, that day last year. Maybe I can explain them to you later. Believe me, though, my dear, I've never been anything more than a man."

She wept awhile at that, not in disappointment. "I, I, I'm so g-glad. I mean, you . . . you'll go to Heaven when you die, but—" But today he was not among her stiff stern Byzantine saints.

"How is your mother?" Havig asked.

He could barely hear: "She . . . has taken the veil. She begs me to do l-l-likewise." The thin fingers twisted together till nails stood white; the look raised to him was terrified. "Should I? I waited for you—to tell me—"

"Don't get me wrong, Doc," Havig said. "The sisters meant well. Their rule was severe, however, especially considering the unsureness when overlords both temporal and spiritual were Catholic. You can imagine, can't you? She loved her God, and books had always been a main part of her life. But hers was the spirit of classical antiquity, as she dreamed that age had been—I never found the heart to disillusion her. And her upbringing—my influence too, no doubt—had turned her early toward the living world. Even lacking that background, a round of prayer and obedience inside the same cloisters, nothing else till death opened the door—was never for her. The ghastly thing which had struck her did not take away her birthright, which was to be a sun-child."

"What'd you do?" I asked.

"I found an elderly couple who'd take her in. They were poor, but I could help them financially; they were childless, which made them extra glad, extra kind to her; and he, a scribe, was a scholar of sorts. It worked out well."

"You made periodic checkups, of course."

Havig nodded. Gentleness touched his mouth. "I had my own projects going," he said. "Still, during the next year or so of my lifespan, the next three of Xenia's, I went back from time to time to visit her. The times got to be oftener and oftener."

chapter 11

The ship was a trimaran, and huge. From the flying bridge, Havig looked across a sweep of deck, beautifully grained hardwood whereon hatches, cargo booms, donkey engines, sunpower screens, and superstructure made a harmonious whole. There was no brightwork; Maurai civilization, poor in metals, must reserve them for the most basic uses. The cabins were shingled. Bougainvillea and trumpet flower vines rioted over them. At each forepeak stood a carven figure representing one of the Trinity—Tanaroa Creator in the middle, a column of abstract symbols; Lesu Haristi holding his cross to starboard; to port, shark-toothed Nan, for death and the dark side of life.

But they were no barbarians who built and crewed this merchantman. The triple hull was designed for ultimate hydrodynamic efficiency. The three great A-frame masts bore sails, true, but these were of esoteric cut and accompanied by vanes which got their own uses out of the wind; the entire rig was continuously readjusted by small motors, which biological fuel cells powered and a computer directed. The personnel were four kanakas and two wahines, who were not overworked.

Captain Rewi Lohannaso held an engineering degree from the University of Wellantoa in N'Zealann. He spoke several languages, and his Ingliss was not the debased dialect of some Merican tribe, but as rich and precise as Havig's native tongue.

A stocky brown man in sarong and bare feet, he said, slowly for the benefit of his passenger who was trying to master the modern speech: "We kept science after technology's world-machine broke down. Our problem was to find new ways to apply that science, on a planet gutted and poisoned. We've not wholly solved it. But we have come far, and I do believe we will go further."

The ocean rolled indigo, turquoise, aquamarine, and aglitter. Waves rushed, wavelets chuckled. Sunlight fell dazzling on sails and on the wings of an albatross. A pod of whales passed majestically across vision. The wind did not pipe in the ears, at the speed of the ship before it, but lulled, brought salty odors, stroked coolness across bare sun-warmed skins. Down on deck, a young man, off duty, drew icy-sweet notes from a bamboo flute, and a girl danced. Their nude bodies were as goodly to see as a cat or a blooded horse.

"That's why you've done a grand thing, Brother Thomas," Lohannaso said. "They'll jubilate when you arrive." He hesitated, "I did not radio for an aircraft to bring you and your goods to the Federation because the Admiralty might have obliged. And . . . frankly, dirigibles are faster, but less reliable than ships. Their engines are feeble; the fireproofing anticatalyst for the hydrogen is experimental."

("I think that brought home to me as much as anything did, the truth about Maurai society in its best days," Havig said to me. "They were—will not be back-to-nature cranks. On the contrary, beneath the easygoing affability, they may well be more development-minded than the USA today. But they won't have the fuel for heavier-than-air craft, anyhow not in their earlier stages; and they won't have the helium for blimps like ours. We squandered so much of everything.")

"Your discovery waited quite a few centuries," Lohannaso went on. "Won't hurt if it waits some extra weeks to get to Wellantoa."

("If I wanted to study the Maurai in depth, to learn what percentage of what Wallis said about them was true and what was lies or blind prejudice, I needed an entrée. Beginning when they first started becoming an important factor in the world, I could follow their history onward. But I had to make that beginning, from scratch. I could pose as a Merican easily enough—among the countless dialects English had split into, mine would pass—but why should they be interested in one more barbarian? And I'd no hope of pretending to be from a semi-civilized community which they had trade relations with. . . . Well, I hit on an answer." Havig grinned. "Can you guess, Doc? No? Okay. Through a twentieth-century dummy I acquired a mess of radioisotopes, like Carbon 14. I left them where they'd be safe—their decay must be real—and moved uptime. There I became Brother Thomas, from an inland stronghold which had preserved a modicum of learning. I'd discovered this trove and decided the Maurai should have it, so carted it myself to the coast. . . . You see? The main thrust of their research was biological. It must be, both because Earth's ecology was in bad need of help, and because life is *the* sunpower converter. But they had no nuclear reactors to manufacture tracer isotopes wholesale. To them, my 'find' was a godsend.")

"Do you think I'll be accepted as a student?" Havig asked anxiously. "It would mean a lot to my people as well as me. But I'm such an outsider—"

Lohannaso laid an arm around his shoulder in the Maurai manner. "Never you sweat, friend. First, we're a trader folk. We pay for value received, and this value is beyond my guessing. Second, we want to spread knowledge, civilization, as wide as we can. We want allies ourselves, trained hands and brains."

"Do you actually hope to convert the whole of mankind?"

"Belay that! Anyhow, if you mean, Do we hope to make everybody into copies of us? The answer is, No. Mind, I'm not in Parliament or Admiralty, but I follow debates and I read the philosophers. One trouble with the old machine culture was that, by its nature, it did force people to become more and more alike. Not only did this fail in the end—disastrously—but to the extent it succeeded, it was a worse disaster." Lohannaso smote the rail with a mighty fist. "Damnation, Thomas! We *need* all the diversity, all the assorted ways of living and looking and thinking, we can get!"

He laughed and finished: "Inside of limits, true. The pirates have to be cleaned up, that sort of job. But otherwise—Well, this's getting too bloody solemn. Almost noon now. Let me shoot the sun and do my arithmetic, then Terai comes on duty and you and I'll go have lunch. You haven't lived till you've sampled my beer."

("I spent more than a year among the early Maurai," Havig told me. "Being eager to spread the gospel, they gave me exactly the sort of education I needed for my purposes. They were dear, merry people—oh, yes, they had their share of bad guys, and human failings and miseries, but on the whole, the Federation in that century was a happy place to be.

("That wasn't true of the rest of the world, of course. Nor of the past. I'd keep time-skipping to twentieth-century Wellington or Honolulu, and catching planes to Istanbul, and going back to see how Xenia was getting on.

("When at last I felt I'd reached the point of diminishing returns, as far as that particular future milieu was concerned, I came once more to Latin Constantinople. Xenia was eighteen. Shortly afterward, we married.")

Of their life together, in the five years of hers which were granted them, he told me little. Well, I haven't much I care to tell either of what really mattered between Kate and me.

He did mention some practical problems. They were tripartite: supporting her decently, getting along in the environment to which she was confined, and staying hidden from the Eyrie.

As for the first, his undertaking wasn't quite simple. He couldn't start a business, in a world of guilds, monopolies, complicated regulations, and folk who even in a metropolis—before the printing press, regular mail service, electronic communications—were as gossipy as villagers. It took him considerable research and effort to establish the *persona* of an agent for a newly formed association of Danish merchant adventurers, more observer and contact man than factor and thus not in competition with the Franks. Finance was the least of his worries; a little gold, carried downtime, went a long way. But he must have a plausible explanation for his money.

As for the second, he thought about moving a good, safe distance off, perhaps to Russia or Western Europe, perhaps to Nicaea where a Byzantine monarchy held out and would, at last, regain Constantinople. But no, there was little good and no safety. The Tartars were coming, and the Holy Inquisition. Sacked and conquered, this great city nevertheless offered as much as any place outside a hopelessly alien Orient; and here Xenia was among familiar scenes, in touch with friends and her mother. Besides, wherever they might go, they would be marked, she a Levantine who called herself a Roman, he something else. Because of his masquerade, they more or less had to buy a house in Pera, where foreigners customarily lived. But that town lay directly across the Golden Horn, with frequent ferries.

As for the third, he kept a low profile, neither conspicuously active nor conspicuously reclusive. He found a new pseudonym, Jon Andersen, and trained Xenia to use it and to be vague about her own origin. Helpfully, his Catholic acquaintances had no interest in her, beyond wondering why Ser Jon had handicapped himself by marrying a heretical Greek. If he must have her, why not as a concubine?

"How much of the truth did you tell Xenia?" I inquired.

"None." His brows bent. "That hurt, not keeping secrets but lying to her. It wouldn't have been safe for her to know, however, supposing she could've grasped the idea . . . would it? She was always so open-hearted. Hard enough for her to maintain the deceptions I insisted on, like the new identity I claimed I needed if I was to work for a new outfit. No, she accepted me for what I said I was, and didn't ask about my affairs once she realized that when I was with her I didn't want to think about them. *That* was true."

"But how did you explain her rescue?"

"I said I'd prayed to my patron saint, who'd evidently responded in striking fashion. Her memory of the episode was blurred by horror and bewilderment; she had no trouble believing." He winced. "It hurt me also, to see her light candles and plead like a well-behaved child for the baby of her own that I knew we could never have."

"Hm, apropos religion, did she turn Catholic, or you go through the motions of conversion to Orthodoxy?"

"No. I'd not ask her to change. There has not been a soul less hypocritical than Xenia. To me, it'd have been a minor fib, but I had to stay halfway respectable in the eyes of the Italians, Normans, and French; otherwise we could never have maintained ourselves at a reasonable standard. No, we found us an Eastern priest who'd perform the rite, and a Western bishop who'd grant me dispensation, for, hm, an honorarium. Xenia didn't care. She had principles, but she was tolerant and didn't expect I'd burn in hell, especially if a saint had once aided me. Besides, she was deliriously happy." He smiled. "I was the same, at first and most of the time afterward."

Their house was modest, but piece by piece she furnished and ornamented it with the taste which had been her father's. From its roof you looked across crowded Pera and ships upon the Golden Horn, till Constantinople rose in walls and towers and domes, seeming at this distance nearly untouched. Inland reached countryside where she loved being taken on excursions.

They kept three servants, not many in an age when labor to do was abundant and labor to hire came cheap. Havig got along well with his groom, a raffish Cappadocian married to the cook, and Xenia spoiled their children. Housemaids came and went, themselves taking considerable of the young wife's attention; our machinery today spares us more than physical toil. Xenia did her own gardening, till the patio and a small yard behind the house became a fairyland. Otherwise she occupied herself with needlework, for which she had unusual talent, and the books he kept bringing her, and her devotions, and her superstitions.

"From my viewpoint, the Byzantines were as superstitious as a horse," Havig said. "Magic, divining, guardianship against everything from the Evil Eye to the plague, omens, quack medicines, love philters, you name it, somebody swore by it. Xenia's shibboleth is astrology. Well, what the deuce, that's done no harm—she has the basic common sense to interpret her horoscopes in a reasonable fashion—and we'd go out at night and observe the stars together. You could do that in a city as well as anywhere else, before street lamps and everlasting smog. She is more beautiful by starlight even than daylight. O God, how I must fight myself not to bring her a telescope, just a small one! But it would have been too risky, of course."

"You did a remarkable job of, well, bridging the intellectual gap," I said.

"Nothing remarkable, Doc." His voice, muted, caressed a memory. "She was—is—younger than me, I'd guess by a decade and a half. She's ignorant of a lot that I know. But this works vice versa, remember. She's familiar with the ins and outs of one of the most glorious cosmopolises history will ever see. The people, the folkways, the lore, the buildings, the art, the songs, the books—why, she'd read Greek classics my age never did, that perished in the sack. She'd tell me about them, she'd sit chanting those tremendous lines from Aeschylus or Sophocles, till lightnings ran up and down my backbone; she'd get us both drunk on Sappho, or howling with laughter out of Aristophanes. Knowing what to look for, I often 'happened' to find books in a bazaar . . . downtime."

He stopped for breath. I waited. "The everyday, too," he concluded. "When you finished up in the office, weren't you interested in what Kate had been doing? And then—" he looked away—"there was us. We were always in love."

She used to sing while she went about her household tasks. Riding past the walls to the stable, he would hear those little minor-key melodies, floating out of a window, suddenly sound very happy.

On the whole, he and she were comparatively asocial. Now and then, to keep up his façade, it was necessary to entertain a Western merchant, or for Havig alone to attend a party given by one. He didn't mind. Most of them weren't bad men for their era, and what they told was interesting. But Xenia had all she could do to conceal her terrified loathing. Fortunately, no one expected her to be a twentieth-century-style gracious hostess.

When she stepped from the background and welled and sparkled with life was when Eastern friends came to dinner. Havig got away with that because Jon Andersen, advance man for an extremely distant company, must gather information where he could, hunting crumbs from the tables of Venice and Genoa. He liked those persons himself: scholars, tradesmen, artists, artisans, Xenia's priest, a retired sea captain, and more exotic types, come on diplomacy or business, whom he sought out—Russians, Jews of several origins, an occasional Arab or Turk.

When he must go away, he both welcomed the change and hated the loss of lifespan which might have been shared with Xenia. Fairly frequent absences were needed for him to stay in character. To be sure, a man's office was normally in his house, but Jon Andersen's business would require him not only to go see other men in town, but irregularly to make short journeys by land or sea to various areas.

"Some of that was unavoidable, like accepting an invitation," he told me. "And once in a while, like every man regardless of how thoroughly married, I wanted to drift around on my own for part of a day. But mainly, you realize, I'd go uptime. I didn't—I don't know what good it might do, but I've got this feeling of obligation to uncover the truth. So first I'd project myself to Istanbul, where I kept a false identity with a fat bank account. There/then I'd fly to whatever part of the world was indicated, and head futureward, and continue my study of the Maurai Federation and civilization, its rise, glory, decline, fall, and aftermath."

* * *

Twilight stole slow across the island. Beneath its highest hill, land lay darkling save where firefly lanterns glowed among the homes of sea ranchers; but the waters still glimmered. White against a royal blue which arched westward toward Asia, seen through the boughs of a pine which a hundred years of weather had made into a bonsai, Venus gleamed. On the verandah of Carelo Keajimu's house, smoke drifted fragrant from a censer. A bird sat its perch and sang that intricate, haunting repertoire of melodies for which men had created it; yet this bird was no cageling, it had a place in the woods.

The old man murmured: "Aye, we draw to an end. Dying hurts. Nonetheless the forefathers were wise who in their myths made Nan coequal with Lesu. A thing which endured forever would become unendurable. Death opens a way, for peoples as well as for people."

He fell silent where he knelt beside his friend, until at last he said: "What you relate makes me wonder if we did not stamp our sigil too deeply."

("I'd followed his life," Havig told me. "He began as a brilliant young philosopher who went into statecraft. He finished as an elder statesman who withdrew to become a philosopher. Then I decided he could join you, as one of the two normal-time human beings I dared trust with my secret.

("You see, I'm not wise. I can skim the surface of destiny for information; but can I interpret, can I understand? How am I to know what should be done, or what can be done? I've scuttled around through a lot of years; but Carelo Keajimu lived, worked, thought to the depths of ninety unbroken ones. I needed his help.")

"That is," Havig said, "you feel that, well, one element of your culture is too strong, at the expense of too much else, in the next society?"

"From what you have told me, yes." His host spent some minutes in rumination. They did not seem overly long. "Or, rather, do you not have the feeling of a strange dichotomy . . . uptime, as you say . . . between two concepts which our Maurai ideal was to keep in balance?"

Science, rationality, planning, control. Myth, the liberated psyche, man an organic part of a nature whose rightness transcends knowledge and wisdom.

"It seems to me, from what you tell, that the present overvaluation of machine technology is a passing rage," Keajimu said. "A reaction, not unjustified. We Maurai grew overbearing. Worse, we grew self-righteous. We made that which had once been good into an idol, and thereby allowed what good was left to rot out of it. In the name of preserving cultural diversity, we tried to freeze whole races into shapes which were at best merely quaint, at worst grotesque and dangerous anachronisms. In the name of preserving ecology, we tried to ban work which could lay a course for the stars. No wonder the Ruwenzorya openly order research on a thermonuclear powerplant! No wonder disaffection at home makes us impotent to stop that!"

Again a quietness, until he continued: "But according to your report, Jack my friend, this is a spasm. Afterward the bulk of mankind will reject scientism, will reject science itself and only keep what ossified technology is needful to maintain the world. They will become ever more inward-turning, contemplative, mystical; the common man will look to the sage for enlightenment, who himself will look into himself. Am I right?"

"I don't know," Havig said. "I have that impression, but nothing more than the impression. Mostly, you realize, I don't understand so much as the languages. One or two I can barely puzzle out, but I've never had the time to spare for gaining anything like fluency. It's taken me years of lifespan to learn what little I have learned about you Maurai. Uptime, they're further removed from me."

"And the paradox is deepened," Keajimu said, "by the contrasting sights you have seen. In the middle of a pastoral landscape, spires which hum and shimmer with enigmatic energies. Noiseless through otherwise empty skies glide enormous ships which seem to be made less of metal than of force. And . . . the symbols on a statue, in a book, chiseled across a lintel, revealed by the motion of a hand . . . they are nothing you can comprehend. You cannot imagine where they came from. Am I right?"

"Yes," Havig said miserably. "Carelo, what should I do?"

"I think you are at a stage where the question is, What should I learn?"

"Carelo, I, I'm a single man trying to see a thousand years. I can't! I just, well, feel this increasing doubt . . . that the Eyrie could possibly bring forth those machine aspects. . . . Then what will?"

Keajimu touched him, a moth-wing gesture. "Be calm. A man can do but little. Enough if that little be right."

"What's right? *Is* the future a tyranny of a few technic masters over a humankind that's turned lofty-minded and passive because this world holds nothing except wretchedness? If that's true, what can be done?"

"As a practical politician, albeit retired," Keajimu said with that sudden dryness which could always startle Havig out of a mood, "I suspect you are overlooking the more grisly possibilities. Plain despotism can be outlived. But we Maurai, in our concentration on biology, may have left a heritage worse than the pain it forestalls."

"What?" Havig tensed on his straw mat.

"Edged metal may chop firewood or living flesh," Keajimu declared. "Explosives may clear away rubble or inconvenient human beings. Drugs—well, I will tell you this is a problem that currently troubles our government in its most secret councils. We have chemicals which do more than soothe or stimulate. Under their influence, the subject comes to believe whatever he is told. In detail. As you do in a dream, supplying every necessary bit of color or sound, happiness or fear, past or future. . . . To what extent dare we administer these potions to our key troublemakers?

"I am almost glad to learn that the hegemony of the Federation will go under before this issue becomes critical. The guilt cannot, therefore, be ours." Keajimu bowed toward Havig. "But you, poor time wanderer, you must think beyond the next century. Come, this evening know peace. Observe the stars tread forth, inhale the incense, hear the songbird, feel the breeze, be one with Earth."

I sat alone over a book in my cottage in Senlac, November 1969. The night outside was brilliantly clear and ringingly cold. Frostflowers grew on my windowpanes.

A Mozart symphony lilted from a record player, and the words of Yeats were on my lap, and a finger or two of scotch stood on the table by my easy chair, and sometimes a memory crossed my mind and smiled at me. It was a good hour for an old man.

Knuckles thumped the door. I said an uncharitable word, hauled my body up, constructed excuses while I crossed the rug. My temper didn't improve when Fiddlesticks slipped between my ankles and nearly tripped me. I only kept the damn cat because he had been Kate's. A kitten when she died, he was now near his ending—

As I opened the door, winter flowed in around me. The ground beyond was not snow-covered, but it was frozen. Upon it stood a man who shivered in his inadequate topcoat. He was of medium height, slim, blond, sharp-featured. His age was hard to guess, though furrows were deep in his face.

Half a decade without a sight of him had not dimmed my memories. "Jack!" I cried. A wave of faintness passed through me.

He entered, shut the door, said in a low and uneven voice, "Doc, you've got to help me. My wife is dying."

chapter 12

"Chills and fever, chest pain, cough, sticky reddish sputum . . . yes, sounds like lobar pneumonia," I nodded. "What's scarier is that development of headache, backache, and stiff neck. Could be meningitis setting in."

Seated on the edge of a chair, mouth writhing, Havig implored, "What to do? An antibiotic—"

"Yes, yes. I'm not enthusiastic about prescribing for a patient I'll never see, and letting a layman give the treatment. I would definitely prefer to have her in an oxygen tent."

"I could ferry—" he began, and slumped. "No. A big enough gas container weighs too much."

"Well, she's young," I consoled him. "Probably streptomycin will do the trick." I was on my feet, and patted his stooped back. "Relax, son. You've got time, seeing as how you can return to the instant you left her."

"I'm not sure if I do," he whispered; and this was when he told me everything that had happened.

In the course of it, fear struck me and I blurted my confession. More than a decade back, in conversation with a writer out California way, I had not been able to resist passing on those hints Havig had gotten about the Maurai epoch on his own early trips thence. The culture intrigued me, what tiny bit I knew; I thought this fellow, trained in speculation, might interpret some of the puzzles and paradoxes. Needless to say, the information was presented as sheer playing with ideas. But presented it was, and when he asked my permission to use it in some stories, I'd seen no reason not to agree.

"They were published," I said miserably. "In fact, in one of them he even predicted what you'd discover later, that the Maurai would mount an undercover operation against an underground attempt to build a fusion generator. What if an Eyrie agent gets put on the track?"

"Do you have copies?" Havig demanded.

I did. He skimmed them. A measure of relief eased the lines in his countenance. "I don't think we need worry," he said. "He's changed names and other items; as for the gaps in what you fed him, he's guessed wrong more often than right. If anybody who knows the future should chance to read this, it'll look at most like one of science fiction's occasional close-to-target hits." His laugh rattled. "Which are made on the shotgun principle, remember! . . . But I doubt anybody will. These stories never had wide circulation. They soon dropped into complete obscurity. Time agents wouldn't try to scan the whole mass of what gets printed. Assuredly, Wallis's kind of agents never would."

After a moment: "In a way, this reassures me. I begin to think I've been overanxious tonight. Since nothing untoward has happened thus far to you or your relative, it scarcely will. You've doubtless been checked up on, and dismissed as of no particular importance to my adult self. That's a major reason I've let a long time pass since our last meeting, Doc—your safety. This other Anderson—why, I've never met him at all. He's a connection of a connection."

Again a silence until, grimly: "They haven't even tried to strike at me through my mother, or bait a trap with her. I suppose they figure that's too obvious, or too risky in this era they aren't familiar with—or too something-or-other—to be worthwhile. Stay discreet, and you should be okay. But you've got to help me!"

—Night was grizzled with dawn when at last I asked: "Why come to me? Surely your Maurai have more advanced medicine."

"Yeah. Too advanced. Nearly all of it preventive. They consider drugs as first aid. So, to the best of my knowledge, theirs are no better than yours for something like Xenia's case."

I rubbed my chin. The bristles were stiff and made a scratchy noise. "Always did suspect there's a natural limit to chemotherapy," I remarked. "Damn, I'd like to know what they do about virus diseases!"

Havig stirred stiffly. "Well, give me the ampoules and hypodermic and I'll be on my way," he said.

"Easy, easy," I ordered. "Remember, I'm no longer in practice. I don't keep high-powered materials around. We've got to wait till the pharmacy opens—no, you will not hop ahead to that minute! I want to do a bit of thinking and studying. A different antibiotic might be indicated; streptomycin can have side effects which you'd be unable to cope with. Then you need a little teaching. I'll bet you've never made an injection, let alone nursed a convalescent. And first off, we both require a final dose of scotch and a long snooze."

"The Eyrie—"

"Relax," I said again to the haggard man in whom I could see the despair-shattered boy. "You just got through deciding those bandits have lost interest in me. If they were onto your arrival at this point in time, they'd've been here to collar you already. Correct?"

His head moved heavily up and down. "Yeah. I s'pose."

"I sympathize with your caution, but I do wish you'd consulted me at an earlier stage of your wife's illness."

"Don't I? . . . At first, seemed like she'd only gotten a bad cold. They're tougher then than we are today. Infants die like flies. Parents don't invest our kind of love in a baby, not till it's past the first year or two. By the same token, though, if you survive babyhood the chances are you'll throw off later sicknesses. Xenia didn't go to bed, in spite of feeling poorly, till overnight—" He could not finish.

"Have you checked her personal future?" I asked.

The sunken eyes sought me while they fought off sleep. The exhausted voice said: "No. I've never dared."

Nor will I ever know how well-founded was his fear of foreseeing when Xenia would die. Did ignorance save his freedom, or merely his illusion of freedom? I know nothing except that he stayed with me for a pair of days, dutifully resting his body and training his hands, until he could minister to his wife. In the end he said goodbye, neither of us sure we would come together again; and he drove his rented car to the city airport, and caught his flight to Istanbul, and went pastward with what I had given him, and was captured by the Eyrie men.

It was likewise November in 1213. Havig had chosen that month out of 1969 because he knew it would be inclement, his enemies not likely to keep a stakeout around my cottage. Along the Golden Horn, the weather was less extreme. However, a chill had blown down from Russia, gathering rain as it crossed the Black Sea. For defense, houses had nothing better than charcoal braziers; hypocausts were too expensive for this climate and these straitened times. Xenia's slight body shivered, day after day, until the germs awoke in her lungs.

Havig frequently moved his Istanbul lair across both

miles and years. As an extra safety factor, he always kept it on the far side of the strait from his home. Thus he must take a creaky-oared ferry, and walk from the dock up streets nearly deserted. In his left hand hung the chronolog, in his right was clutched a flat case containing the life of his girl. Raindrops spattered out of a lowering grayness, but the mists were what drenched his Frankish cloak, tunic, and trousers, until they clung to his skin and the cold gnawed inward. His footfalls resounded hollow on slickened cobblestones. Gutters gurgled. Dim amidst swirling vapors, he glimpsed himself hurrying down to the waterfront, hooded against the damp, too frantic to notice himself. He would have been absent a quarter hour when he returned to Xenia. Though the time was about three o'clock in the afternoon, already darkness seeped from below.

His door was closed, the shutters were bolted, wan lamplight shone through cracks.

He knocked, expecting the current maid—Eulalia, was that her name?—to lift the latch and grumble him in. She'd be surprised to see him back this soon, but the hell with her.

Hinges creaked. Gloom gaped beyond. A man in Byzantine robe and beard occupied the doorway. The shotgun in his grasp bulked monstrous. "Do not move, Havig," he said in English. "Do not try to escape. Remember, we hold the woman."

Save for an ikon of the Virgin, their bedroom was decorated in gaiety. Seen by what light trickled in a glazed window, the painted flowers and beasts jeered. It was wrong that a lamb should gambol above Xenia where she lay. She was so small and thin in her nightgown. Skin, drawn tight across the frail bones, was like new-fallen snow dappled with blood. Her mouth was dry, cracked, and gummed. Only the hair, tumbling loose over her bosom, and the huge frightened eyes had luster.

The man in East Roman guise, whom Havig did not know, held his left arm in a practiced grip. Juan Mendoza had the right, and smirked each time he put backward pressure on the elbow joint. He was dressed in Western style, as was Waclaw Krasicki, who stood at the bedside.

"Where are the servants?" Havig asked mechanically.

"We shot them," Mendoza said.

"What—"

"They didn't recognize a gun, so that wouldn't scare them. We couldn't let a squawk warn you. Shut up."

The shock of knowing they were dead, the hope that the children had been spared and that an orphanage might take them in, struck Havig dully, like a blow on flesh injected with painkiller. Xenia's coughing tore him too much.

"Hauk," she croaked, "no, Jon, Jon—" Her hands lifted toward him, strengthless, and his were caught immobile.

Krasicki's broad visage had noticeably aged. Years of his lifespan must have passed, uptime, downtime, everywhen an outrage was to be engineered. He said in frigid satisfaction: "You may be interested to know what a lot of work went on for how long, tracking you down. You've cost us, Havig."

"Why . . . did . . . you bother?" the prisoner got out.

"You did not imagine we could leave you alone, did you? Not just that you killed men of ours. You're not an ignorant lout, you're smart and therefore dangerous. I've been giving this job my personal attention."

Havig thought drearily: *What an overestimate of me.*

"We must know what you've been doing," Krasicki continued. "Take my advice and cooperate."

"How did you—?"

"Plenty of detective work. We reasoned, if a Greek family was worth to you what you did, you'd keep in touch with them. You covered your trail well, I admit. But given our limited personnel, and the problems in working here, and everything else we had to do throughout history—you needn't feel too smug about your five-year run. Naturally, when we did close in, we chose this moment for catching you. The whole neighborhood knows your wife is seriously ill. We waited till you went out, expecting you'd soon be back." Krasicki glanced at Xenia. "And cooperative, no?"

She shuddered and barked, as an abandoned dog had barked while her father was slain. Blood colored the mucus she cast up.

"Christ!" Havig screamed. "Let me go! Let me treat her!"

"Who are they, Jon?" she pleaded. "What do they want? Where is your saint?"

"Besides," Mendoza said, "Pat Moriarty was a friend of mine." He applied renewed pressure, barely short of fracturing.

Through the ragged darknesses which pain rolled across him, Havig heard Krasicki: "If you behave, if you come along with us, not making trouble, okay, we'll leave her in peace. I'll even give her a shot from that kit I guess you went to fetch."

"That . . . isn't . . . enough. . . . Please, please—"

"It's as much as she'll get. I tell you, we've already wasted whole man-years on your account. Don't make us waste more, and take added risks. Look, would you rather we broke her arms?"

Havig sagged and wept.

Krasicki kept his promise, but his insertion of the needle was clumsy and Xenia shrieked. "It's well, it's well, my darling, everything's well, the saints watch over you." Havig cried from the far side of a chasm which roared. To

Krasicki: "Listen, let me say goodbye to her, you've got to, I'll do anything you ask if you let me say goodbye."

Krasicki shrugged. "Okay, if you're quick."

Mendoza and the other man kept their hold on Havig while he stooped above his girl. "I love you," he told her, not knowing if she really heard him through the fever and terror. The mummy lips that his touched were not those he remembered.

"All right," Krasicki said, "let's go."

Uptime bound, Havig lost awareness of the men on either side of him. They had substance to his senses, like his own body, but only the shadow-flickers in the room were real. He saw her abandoned, reaching and crying; he saw her become still; he saw someone who must have grown worried and broken down the door step in, days later; he saw confusion, and then the chamber empty, and then strangers in it.

So he might have resisted, willed himself to stay in normal time at their first stop for air, an inertness which his captors could not move. But there are ways to erode any will. Better not arrive at the Eyrie crippled alike in body and spirit, ready for whatever might occur to Caleb Wallis. Better keep the capability of revenge.

That thought was vague. The whole of him was drowned in her death. He scarcely noticed how the shadows shifted—the house which had been hers and his torn down for a larger, which caught fire when the Turks took Pera, and was succeeded by building after building filled with faces and faces and faces, until the final incandescence and the drifting radioactive ash—nor their halt among ruins, their flight across the ocean, their further journey to that future where the Sachem waited. In him was nothing except Xenia, who saw him vanish and lay back to die alone, unshriven.

* * *

While summer blanketed the Eyrie in heat and brazen light, the tower room where Havig was confined stored cool dimness in its bricks. It was bare save for a washstand, a toilet, a mattress, and two straight chairs. A single window gave upon the castle, the countryside, the peasants at labor for their masters. When you had looked out into yonder sunshine, you were blind for a while.

A wire rope, welded at the ends, stretched five feet from a ring locked around his ankle to a staple in the wall. That sufficed. A time traveler bore along whatever was in direct contact with him, such as clothing. In effect, Havig would have had to carry away the entire keep. He did not try.

"Sit down, do sit down," Caleb Wallis urged.

He had planted his broad bottom in one of the chairs, beyond reach of his prisoner. Black, epauletted uniform, neatly combed gingery whiskers, bare pate were an assertion of lordship over Havig's grimed archaic clothes, stubbly jaws, bloodshot and murk-encircled eyes.

Wallis waved his cigar. "I'm not necessarily mad at you," he said. "In fact, I kind of admire your energy, your cleverness. I'd like to recall them to my side. That's how come I ordered the boys to let you rest before this interview. I hope the chow was good? Do sit down."

Havig obeyed. He had not ceased to feel numb. During the night he had dreamed about Xenia. They were bound somewhere on a great trimaran whose sails turned into wings and lifted them up among stars.

"We're private here," Wallis said. An escort waited beyond the door, which stood thick and shut. "You can talk free."

"Supposing I don't?" Havig replied.

The eyes which confronted him were like bullets. "You will. I'm a patient man, but I don't aim to let you monkey any further with my destiny. You're alive because I think maybe you can give us some compensation for the harm you've done, the trouble you've caused. For instance, you know your way around in the later twentieth century. And you have money there. That could be mighty helpful. It better be."

Havig reached inside his tunic. He thought dully: *How undramatic that a new-made widower, captive and threatened with torture, should be unbathed, and on that account should stink and itch.* He'd remarked once to Xenia that her beloved Classical poets left out those touches of animal reality; and she'd shown him passages in Homer, the playwrights, the hymners, oh, any number of them to prove him wrong; her forefinger danced across the lines, and bees hummed among her roses. . . .

"I gather you were keeping a wench in Constantinople, and she fell sick and had to be let go," Wallis said. "Too bad. I sympathize, kind of. Still, you know, lad, in a way you brought it on yourself. And on her." The big bald head swayed. "Yes, you did. I'm not telling you God has punished you. That could be, but nature does give people what they deserve, and it is not fitting for a proper white man to bind himself to a female like that. She was Levantine, you know. Which means mongrel—Armenian, Asiatic, hunky, spig, Jew, probably a touch of nigger—" Again Wallis's cigar moved expansively. "Mind, I've nothing against you boys having your fun," he said with a jovial wink. "No, no. Part of your pay, I guess, sampling damn near anyone you want, when you want her, and no nonsense afterward out of her or anybody else." He scowled. "But you, Jack, you *married* this'n."

Havig tried not to listen. He failed. The voice boomed in on him:

"There's more wrongness in that than meets the eye. It's what I call a symbolic thing to do. You bring yourself down, because a mixed-breed can't possibly be raised to your level. And so you bring down your whole race." The tone harshened. "Don't you understand? It's always been the curse of the white man. Because he is more intelligent and sensitive, he opens himself to those who hate him. They divide him against himself, they feed him lies, they slide their slimy way into control of his own homelands, till he finds he's gotten allied with his natural enemy against his brother. Oh, yes, yes, I've studied your century, Jack. That's when the conspiracy flowered into action, wrecked the world, unlocked the gates for Mong and Maurai. . . . You know what I think is one of the most awful tragedies of all time? When two of the greatest geniuses the white race ever produced, its two possible saviors from the Slav and the Chinaman, were lured into war on different sides. Douglas MacArthur and Adolf Hitler."

Havig knew—an instant later, first with slight surprise, next with a hot satisfaction—that he had spat on the floor and snapped: "If the General ever heard you say that, I wouldn't give this for your life, Wallis! Not that it's worth it anyway."

Surprisingly, or maybe not, he provoked no anger. "You prove exactly what I was talking about." The Sachem's manner verged on sorrow. "Jack, I've got to make you see the plain truth. I know you have sound instincts. They've only been buried under a stack of cunning lies. You've *seen* that nigger empire in the future, and yet you can't see what ought to be done, what must be done, to put mankind back on the right evolutionary road."

Wallis drew upon his cigar till its end glowed beacon-red, exhaled pungent smoke, and added benign-voiced: "Of course, you're not yourself today. You've lost this girl you cared about, and like I told you, I do sympathize." Pause. "However, she'd be long dead by now regardless, wouldn't she?"

He grew utterly intense. "Everybody dies," he said.

"Except us. I don't believe we travelers need to. You can be among us. You can live forever."

Havig resisted the wish to reply. "I don't want to, if you're included in the deal." He waited.

"They're bound to find immortality, far off in the world we're building," Wallis said. "I'm convinced. I'll tell you something. This is confidential, but either I can trust you eventually or you die. I've been back to the close of Phase One, more thoroughly than I'd been when I wrote the manual. You remember I'll be old then. Sagging cheeks, rheumy eyes, shaky liver-spotted hands . . . not pleasant to see yourself old, no, not pleasant." He stiffened. "This trip I learned something new. At the end, I am going to disappear. I will never be seen any more, aside from my one short visit I've already paid to Phase Two. Never. And likewise a number of my chief lieutenants. I didn't get every name of theirs—no use spending lifespan on that—but I wouldn't be bowled over if you turned out to be among them."

Faintly, the words pricked Havig's returning apathy. "What do you suppose will have happened?" he asked.

"Why, the thing I wrote about," Wallis exulted. "The reward. Our work done, we were called to the far future and made young forever. Like unto gods."

In the sky outside, a crow cawed.

The trumpet note died from Wallis' words. "I hope you'll be included, Jack," he said. "I do. You're a go-getter. I don't mind admitting your talk about your experiences on your own hook in Constantinople was what gave Krasicki the idea of our raid. And you did valuable work there, too, before you went crazy. That was our best haul to date. It's given us what we need to expand into the period. Believe me, Caleb Wallis is not ungrateful.

"Sure," he purred, "you were shocked. You came new to the hard necessities of our mission. But what about Hiroshima, hey? What about some poor homesick Hessian lad, sold into service, dying of lead in his belly for the sake of American independence? Come to that, Jack, what about the men, your comrades in arms, who you killed?

"Let's set them against this girl you happened to get infatuated with. Let's chalk off your services to us against the harm you've done. Even-Steven, right? Okay. You must've been busy in the years that followed. You must've collected a lot of information. How about sharing it? And leading us to your money, signing it over? Earning your way back into our brotherhood?"

Sternness: "Or do you want the hot irons, the pincers, the dental drills, the skilled attentions of professionals you know we got—till what's left of you obliges me in the hope I'll let it die?"

Night entered first the room, then the window. Havig gazed stupidly at the recorder and the supper which had been brought him, until he could no longer see them.

He ought to yield, he thought. Wallis could scarcely be lying about the future of the Eyrie. If you can't lick 'em, join 'em, and hope to be an influence for mercy, in the name of Xenia's timid ghost.

Yet if—for example—Wallis learned about the Maurai psychodrugs, which the Maurai themselves dreaded, and sent men uptime—

Well, Julius Caesar butchered and subjugated to further his political career. In the process he laid the keel of Western civilization, which in its turn gave the world Chartres Cathedral, St. Francis of Assisi, penicillin, Bach, the Bill of Rights, Rembrandt, astronomy, Shakespeare, an end to chattel slavery, Goethe, genetics, Einstein, woman suffrage, Jane Addams, man's footprints on the moon and man's vision turned to the stars . . . yes, also the nuclear warhead and totalitarianism, the automobile and the Fourth

Crusade, but on the whole, on balance, in an aspect of eternity—

Dared he, mere Jack Havig, stand against an entire tomorrow for the sake of a little beloved dust?

Could he? An executioner would be coming to see if he had put something on tape.

He had better keep in mind that Jack Havig counted for no more in eternity than Doukas Manasses, or Xenia, or anybody.

Except: he did not have to give the enemy a free ride. He could make them burn more of their lifespans. For whatever that might be worth.

A hand shook him. He groped his way out of uneasy sleep. The palm clapped onto his mouth. In blackness: "Be quiet, you fool," whispered Leonce.

chapter 13

A pencil flashlight came to life. Its beam probed until the iron sheened on Havig's ankle. "Ah," she breathed. "That's how they bottle you? Like I reckoned. Hold this." She thrust the tube at him. Dizzy, rocked by his heartbeat, scarcely believing, he could not keep it steady. She said a bad word, snatched it back, took it between her teeth, and crouched over him. A hacksaw began to grate.

"Leonce—my dear, you shouldn't—" he stammered.

She uttered an angry grunt. He swallowed and went silent. Stars glistened in the window.

When the cable parted, leaving him with only the circlet, he tottered erect. She snapped off the light, stuck the tube in her shirt pocket—otherwise, he had glimpsed, she wore jeans and hiking shoes, gun and knife—and grasped him by the upper arms. "Listen," she hissed. "You skip ahead to sunrise. Let 'em bring you breakfast before you return to now. Got me? We want 'em to think you escaped at a later hour. Can you carry it off? If not, you're dead."

"I'll try," he said faintly.

"Good." Her kiss was brief and hard. "Be gone."

Havig moved uptime at a cautious pace. When the window turned gray he emerged, arranged his tether to look uncut to a casual glance, and waited. He had never spent a longer hour.

A commoner guard brought in a tray of food and coffee. "Hello," Havig said inanely.

He got a surly look and a warning: "Eat fast. They want to talk to you soon."

For a sick instant, Havig thought the man would stay and watch. But he retired. After the door had slammed, Havig must sit down for a minute; his knees would not upbear him.

Leonce— He gulped the coffee. Will and strength resurged. He rose to travel back nightward.

The light-gleam alerted him to his moment. As he entered normal time, he heard a hoarse murmur across the room: "—Can you carry it off? If not, you're dead."

"I'll try."

"Good." Pause. "Be gone."

He heard the little rush of air filling a vacuum where his body had been, and knew he had departed. "Here I am," he called low.

"Huh? Ah!" She must see better in the dark than he, because she came directly to him. "All 'kay?"

"Yes. Maybe."

"No chatter," she commanded. "They may decide to check these hours, 'spite of our stunt. Here, hold my hand an' slip downtime. Don't hurry yourself. I know we'll make it. I just don't want 'em to find out how."

Part of the Eyrie's training was in such simultaneous travel. Each felt a resistance if starting to move "faster" or "slower" than the partner, and adjusted the chronokinetic rate accordingly.

A few nights earlier, the chamber was unoccupied, the door unlocked. They walked down shadow stairs, across shadow courtyard, through gates which, in this period of unchallenged reign, were usually left open. At intervals they must emerge for breath, but that could be in the dark. Beyond the lowered drawbridge, Leonce lengthened her stride. Havig wondered why she didn't simply go to a day before the castle existed, until he realized the risk was too great of encountering others in the vicinity. A lot of men went hunting in the primeval forest which once grew here.

Dazed with fatigue and grief, he would do best to follow her lead. She'd gotten him free, hadn't she?

She really had. He needed a while to conceive of that.

They sat in the woods, one summer before Columbus was born. The trees, oak and elm and birch mingled together, were gigantic; their fragrance filled the air, their leaves cast green shadows upon the nearly solid underbrush around them. Somewhere a woodpecker drummed and a bluejay scolded. The fire glowed low which Leonce had built. On an improvised spit roasted a grouse she had brought down out of a thousandfold flock which they startled when they arrived.

"I can never get over it," she said, "what a wonderful world this is before machine man screws things up. I don't think a lot o' the High Years any more. I've been then too often."

Havig, leaning against a bole, had a brief eerie sense of *déjà vu*. The cause came to him: this setting was not unlike that almost a millennium hence, when he and she— He regarded her more closely than hitherto. Mahogany hair in a kind of Dutch bob, suntan faded, the Skula's weasel skull left behind and the big body in boyish garb, she might have come straight from his home era. Her English had lost most of the Glacier accent, too. Of course, she still went armed, and her feline gait and haughty bearing hadn't changed.

"How long for you?" he inquired.

"Since you left me in Paris? 'Bout three years." She frowned at the bird, reached and turned it above the coals.

"I'm sorry. That was a shabby way to treat you. Why did you want to spring me?"

Her scowl deepened. "S'pose you tell me what happened."

"You don't know?" he exclaimed in amazement. "For heaven's sake, if you weren't sure why I was under arrest, how could you be sure I didn't deserve—"

"Talk, will you?"

The story stumbled forth, in bare outline. Now and then, during it, the tilted eyes sought him, but her countenance remained expressionless. At the end she said: "Well, seems my hunch was right. I haven't thrown away much. Was gettin' more an' more puked at that outfit, as I saw how it works."

She might have offered a word for Xenia, he thought, and therefore he matched her brusqueness: "I didn't believe you'd object to a spot of fighting and robbery."

"Not if they're honest, strength 'gainst strength, wits 'gainst wits. But those . . . jackals . . . they pick on the helpless. An' for sport more'n for gain." In a kind of leashed savagery, she probed the fowl with her knife point. A drop of fat hit the coals; yellow flame sputtered and flared. " 'Sides, what's the sense o' the whole business? Why *should* we try to fasten machines back on the world? So Cal Wallis can be promoted to God j.g?"

"When you learned I'd been located and was being held, that touched off the rebellion which had been gathering in you?" Havig asked.

She didn't reply directly. "I went downtime, like you'd guess, found when the room was empty, went uptime to you. First, though, I'd spent some days future o' that, not to seem involved in your escape. Ha, ever'body was runnin' 'round like guillotined chickens! I planted the notion you must've co-opted a traveler while you were in the past." The broad shoulders lifted and dropped. "Well, the hooraw blew over. Evidently it didn't seem worth mentionin' to the earlier Wallis, on his inspection tour. Why admit a failure? His next appearance beyond your vanishment was years ahead, an' nothin' awful had happened meanwhile. You didn't matter. Nor will I, when I never return from my furlough. I s'pose they'll reckon I died in an accident." She chuckled. "I do like sports cars, an' drive like a bat out o' Chicago."

"In spite of, uh, opposing a restoration of machine society?" Havig wondered.

"Well, we can enjoy it while we got it, can't we, whether or not it'll last or ought to?" She observed him steadily, and her tone bleakened. "That's 'bout all we can do, you an' me. Find ourselves some nice hidey-holes, here an' there in space-time. Because we're sure not goin' to upset the Eyrie."

"I'm not certain its victory is predestined," Havig said. "Maybe wishful thinking on my part. After what I've seen, however—" His earnestness helped cover the emptiness in him where Xenia had been. "Leonce, you do wrong to put down science and technology. They can be misused, but so can everything. Nature never has been in perfect balance—there are many more extinct species than live—and primitive man was quite as destructive as modern. He simply took longer to use up his environment. Probably Stone Age hunters exterminated the giant mammals of the Pleistocene. Certainly farmers with sickles and digging sticks wore out what started as the Fertile Crescent. And nearly all mankind died young, from causes that are preventable when you know how. . . . The Maurai will do more than rebuild the foundation of Earth's life. They'll make the first attempt ever to *create* a balanced environment. And that'll only be possible because they do have the scientific knowledge and means."

"Don't seem like they'll succeed."

"I can't tell. That mysterious farther future . . . it's got to be studied." Havig rubbed his eyes. "Later, later. Right now I'm too tired. Let me borrow your Bowie after lunch and cut some boughs to sleep on for a week or three."

She moved, then, to come kneel before him and lay one hand on his neck, run fingers of the other through his hair. "Poor Jack," she murmured. "I been kind o' short with you, haven't I? Forgive. Was a strain on me also, this gettin' away an'— Sure, sleep. We have peace. Today we have peace."

"I haven't thanked you for what you did," he said awkwardly. "I'll never be able to thank you."

"You bugbrain!" She cast arms around him. "Why do you think I hauled you out o' there?"

"But—but—Leonce, I've seen my wife die—"

"Sure," she sobbed. "How I . . . I'd like to go back . . . an' meet that girl. If she made you happy— Can't be, I know. Well, I'll wait, Jack. As long as needful, I'll wait."

They weren't equipped to stay more than a short while in ancient America. They could have gone uptime, bought gear, ferried it back. But after what they had suffered, no idle idyll was possible for them.

More important was the state of Havig's being. The wound in him healed slowly, but it healed, and left a hard scar: the resolve to make war upon the Eyrie.

He didn't think it was merely a desire for vengeance upon Xenia's murderers. Leonce assumed this, and leagued herself with him because a Glacier woman stood by her man. He admitted that to a degree she was correct. (Is the impulse always evil? It can take the form of exacting justice.) Mainly, he believed that he believed, a brigand gang must be done away with. The ghastlinesses it had already made, and would make, were unchangeable;

but could not the sum of that hurt be stopped from mounting, could not the remoter future be spared?

"A thing to puzzle over," he told Leonce, "is that no time travelers seem to be born in the Maurai era or afterward. They might stay incognito, sure, same as the majority of them probably do in earlier history—too frightened or too crafty to reveal their uniqueness. Nevertheless . . . every single one? Hardly sounds plausible, does it?"

"Did you investigate?" she asked.

They were in a mid-twentieth-century hotel. Kansas City banged and winked around them, early at night. He was avoiding his former resorts until he could be sure that Wallis's men would not discover these. The lamplight glowed soft over Leonce where she sat, knees drawn close to chin, in bed. She wore a translucent peignoir. Otherwise she gave him no sign that she was anything more in her heart than his sisterlike companion. A huntress learns patience, a Skula learns to read souls.

"Yes," he said. "I've told you about Carelo Keajimu. He has connections across the globe. If he can't turn up a traveler, nobody can. And he drew a blank."

"What does this mean?"

"I don't know, except— Leonce, we've got to take the risk. We've got to make an expedition uptime of the Maurai."

Again practical problems consumed lifespan.

Think. One epoch does not suddenly and entirely replace another. Every trend is blurred by numberless countercurrents. Thus, Martin Luther was not the first Protestant in the true sense—doctrinal as well as political—of that word. He was simply the first who made it stick. And his success was built on the failures of centuries, Hussites, Lollards, Albigensians, on and on to the heresies of Christendom's dawn; and those had origins more ancient yet. Likewise, the thermonuclear reactor and associated machines were introduced, and spread widely, while mysticism out of Asia was denying, in millions of minds, that science could answer the questions that mattered.

If you want to study an epoch, in what year do you begin?

You can move through time, but once at your goal, what have you besides your feet for crossing space? Where do you shelter? How do you eat?

It took a number of quick trips futureward to find the start of a plan.

Details are unimportant. On the west coast of thirty-first-century North America, a hybrid Ingliss-Maurai-Spanyol had not evolved too far for Havig to grope his way along in it. He took back a grammar, a dictionary, and assorted reading material. By individual concentration and mutual practice, he and Leonce acquired some fluency.

Enough atomic-powered robot-crewed commerce brought enough visitors from overseas that two more obvious foreigners would attract no undue attention. This was the more true because Sancisco was a favorite goal of pilgrimages; there the guru Duago Samito had had his revelation. Nobody believed in miracles. People did believe that, if you stood on the man-sculptured hills and looked down into the chalice which was the Bay, and let yourself become one with heaven and earth and water, you could hope for insight.

Pilgrims needed no credit account in the financial world-machine. The age was, in its austere fashion, prosperous. A wayside householder could easily spare the food and sleeping room that would earn virtue for him and travelers' tales for his children.

"If you seek the Star Masters—" said the dark, gentle man who housed them one night. "Yes, they keep an outpost nigh. But surely some are in your land."

"We are curious to see if the Star Masters here are like those we know at home," Havig replied. "I have heard they number many kinds."

"Correct. Correct."

"It does not add undue kilometers to our journey."

"You need not walk there. A call will do." Havig's host indicated the holographic communicator which stood in a corner of a room whose proportions were as alien—and as satisfying—to his guests as a Japanese temple would have been to a medieval European or a Gothic church to a Japanese.

"Though I doubt their station is manned at present," he continued. "They do not come often, you know."

"At least we can touch it," Havig said.

The dark man nodded. "Aye. A full-sense savoring . . . aye, you do well. Go in God, then, and be God, happily."

In the morning, after an hour's chanting and meditation, the family returned to their daily round. Father hand-cultivated his vegetable garden; the reason for that seemed more likely depth-psychological than economic. Mother continued her work upon a paramathematical theorem too esoteric for Havig to grasp. Children immersed themselves in an electronic educational network which might be planet-wide and might involve a kind of artificial telepathy. Yet the house was small, unpretentious except for the usual scrimshaw and Oriental sweep of roof, nearly alone in a great tawny hillscape.

Trudging down a dirt road, where dust whoofed around her boots while a many-armed automaton whispered through the sky overhead, Leonce sighed: "You're right. I do not understand these people."

"That could take a lifetime," Havig agreed. "Something new has entered history. It needn't be bad, but it's surely new."

After a space he added: "Has happened before. Could

your paleolithic hunter really understand your neolithic farmer? How much alike were a man who lived under the divine right of kings and a man who lived under the welfare state? I don't always follow your mind, Leonce."

"Nor I yours." She caught his hand. "Let's keep tryin'."

"It seems—" Havig said, "I repeat, it seems—these Star Masters occupy the ultra-mechanized, energy-flashing bases and the enormous flying craft and everything else we've glimpsed which contrasts so sharply with the rest of the Earth. They come irregularly. Otherwise their outposts lie empty. Does sound like time travelers, hey?"

"But they're kind o', well, good. Aren't they?"

"Therefore they can't be Eyrie? Why not? In origin, anyhow. The grandson of a conquering pirate may be an enlightened king." Havig marshaled his thoughts. "True, the Star Masters act differently from what one would expect. As near as I can make out—remember, I don't follow this modern language any more closely than you do, and besides, there are a million taken-for-granted concepts behind it—as near as I can make out, they come to trade: ideas and knowledge more than material goods. Their influence on Earth is subtle but pervasive. My trips beyond this year suggest their influence will grow, till a new civilization—or post-civilization—has arisen which I cannot fathom."

"Don't the locals describe 'em as bein' sometimes human . . . an' sometimes not?"

"I have that impression too. Maybe we've garbled a figure of speech."

"You'll make it out," she said.

He glanced at her. The glance lingered. Sunlight lay on her hair and the tiny drops of sweat across her face. He caught the friendly odor of her flesh. The pilgrim's robe molded itself to long limbs. Timeless above a cornfield, a red-winged blackbird whistled.

"We'll see if we can," he said.

She smiled.

Clustered spires and subtly curved domes were deserted when they arrived. An invisible barrier held them off. They moved uptime. When they glimpsed a ship among the shadows, they halted.

At that point, the vessel had made groundfall. The crew were coming down an immaterial ramp. Havig saw men and women in close-fitting garments which sparkled as if with constellations. And he saw shapes which Earth could never have brought forth, not in the age of the dinosaurs nor in the last age when a swollen red sun would burn her barren.

A shellbacked thing which bore claws and nothing identifiable as a head conversed with a man in notes of music. The man was laughing.

Leonce screamed. Havig barely grabbed her before she was gone, fleeing downtime.

"But don't you see?" he told her, over and over. "Don't you realize the marvel of it?"

And at last he got her to seek night. They stood on a high ridge. Uncountable stars gleamed from horizon to zenith to horizon. Often a meteor flashed. The air was cold, their breath smoked wan, she huddled in his embrace. Quietness enclosed them: "the eternal silence of yonder infinite spaces."

"Look up," he said. "Each of those lights is a sun. Did you think ours is the single living planet in the universe?"

She shuddered. "What we saw—"

"What we saw was different. Magnificently different." He searched for words. His whole youth had borne a vision which hers had known only as a legend. The fact that it was not forever lost sang in his blood. "Where else can newness, adventure, rebirth of spirit, where else can they come from except difference? The age beyond the Maurai is not turned inward on itself. No, it's begun to turn further outward than ever men did before!"

"Tell me," she begged. "Help me."

He found himself kissing her. And they sought a place of their own and were one.

But there are no happy endings. There are no endings of any kind. At most, we are given happy moments.

The morning came when Havig awakened beside Leonce. She slept, warm and silky and musky, an arm thrown across his breast. This time his body did not desert her. His thinking did.

"Doc," he was to tell me, his voice harsh with desperation, "I could not stay where we were—in a kind of Renaissance Eden—I couldn't stay there, or anywhere else, and let destiny happen.

"I *believe* the future has taken a hopeful direction. But how can I be sure? Yes, yes, the name is Jack, not Jesus; my responsibility must end somewhere; but exactly where?

"And even if that was a good eon to be alive in, by what route did men arrive there? Maybe you remember, I once gave you my opinion, Napoleon ought to have succeeded in bringing Europe together. This does not mean Hitler ought to have. The chimney stacks of Belsen say different. What about the Eyrie?"

He roused Leonce. She girded herself to fare beside her man.

They might have visited Carelo Keajimu. But he was, in a way, too innocent. Though he lived in a century of disintegration, the Maurai rule had always been mild, had never provoked our organized unpity. Furthermore, he was too prominent, his lifetime too likely to be watched.

It was insignificant me whom Jack Havig and Leonce of Wahorn sought out.

chapter 14

April 12, 1970. Where I dwelt that was a day of new-springing greenness wet from the night's rain, clouds scudding white before a wind which ruffled the puddles in my driveway, earth cool and thick in my fingers as I knelt and planted bulbs of iris.

Gravel scrunched beneath wheels. A car pulled in, to stop beneath a great old chestnut tree which dominated the lawn. I didn't recognize the vehicle and swore a bit while I rose; it's never pleasant getting rid of salesmen. Then they stepped out, and I knew him and guessed who she must be.

"Doc!" Havig ran to hug me. "God, I'm glad to see you!"

I was not vastly surprised. In the months since last he was here, I had been expecting him back if he lived. But at this minute I realized how much I'd fretted about him.

"How's your wife?" I asked.

The joy died out of his face. "She didn't live. I'll tell you about it . . . later."

"Oh, Jack, I'm sorry—"

"Well, for me it happened a year and a half ago." When

he turned to the rangy redhead approaching us, he could again smile. "Doc, Leonce, you've both heard plenty about each other. Now meet."

Like him, she was careless of my muddy handclasp. I found it at first an unsettling encounter. Never before had I seen someone from out of time; Havig didn't quite count. And, while he hadn't told me much concerning her, enough of the otherness had come through in his narrative. She did not think or act or exist remotely like any woman, any human creature, born into my epoch. Did she?

Yet the huntress, tribal councilor, she-shaman, casual lover and unrepentant killer of—how many?—men, wore an ordinary dress and, yes, nylon stockings and high-heeled shoes, carried a purse, smiled with a deftly lipsticked mouth, and said in English not too different from my own: "How do you do, Dr. Anderson? I have looked forward to this pleasure."

"Come on inside," I said weakly. "Let's get washed and, and I'll make a pot of tea."

Leonce tried hard to stay demure, and failed. While Havig talked she kept leaving her chair, prowling to the windows and peering out at my quiet residential street. "Calm down," he told her at length. "We checked uptime, remember? No Eyrie agents."

"We couldn't check every minute," she answered.

"No, but—well, Doc, about a week hence I'll phone you and ask you if we had any trouble, and you'll tell me no."

"They could be readyin' somethin'," Leonce said.

"Unlikely." Havig's manner was a bit exasperated; obviously they'd been over this ground before. "We're written off. I'm certain of it."

"I s'pose I got nervous habits when I was a girl."

Havig hesitated before he said, "If they are after us, and

onto Doc's being our contact, wouldn't they strike through him? Well, they haven't." To me: "Hard to admit I've knowingly exposed you to a hazard. It's why I avoid my mother."

"That's okay, Jack." I attempted a laugh. "Gives me an interesting hobby in my retirement."

"Well, you will be all right," he insisted. "I made sure."

Leonce drew a sharp breath. For a time nothing spoke except the soughing in the branches outside. A cloud shadow came and went.

"You mean," I said at last, "you verified I'll live quietly till I die."

He nodded.

"You know the date of that," I said.

He sat unmoving.

"Well, don't tell me," I finished. "Not that I'm scared. However, I'd just as soon keep on enjoying myself in the old-fashioned mortal style. I don't envy you—that you can lose a friend twice."

My teakettle whistled.

"And so," I said after hours had gone by, "you don't propose to stay passive? You mean to do something about the Eyrie?"

"If we can," Havig said low.

Leonce, seated beside him, gripped his arm. "What, though?" she almost cried. "I been uptime myself—quick-like, but the place is bigger'n ever, an' I saw Cal Wallis step from an aircraft—they got robotic factories built by then—an' he was gettin' old but he was there." Fingers crooked into talons. "Nobody'd killed the bastard, not in that whole while."

I tamped my pipe. We had eaten, and sat among my books and pictures, and I'd declared the sun sufficiently near a nonexistent yardarm that whiskey might be poured.

But in those two remained no simple enjoyment of a call paid on an old acquaintance, or for her a new one; this had faded, the underlying grief and anger stood forth like stones.

"You have no complete account of the Eyrie's future career," I said.

"Well, we've read Wallis's book and listened to his words," Havig answered. "We don't believe he's lying. His kind of egotist wouldn't, not on such a topic."

"You miss my point." I wagged my pipestem at them. "The question is, Have you personally made a year-by-year inspection?"

"No," Leonce replied. "Originally no reason to, an' now too dangerous." Her gaze steadied on me. She was a bright lass. "You aimin' at somethin', Doctor?"

"Maybe." I scratched a match and got my tobacco lit. The small hearthfire would be a comfort in my hand. "Jack, I've spent a lot of thought on what you told me on your previous visit. That's natural. I have the leisure to think and study and—you've come back in the hope I might have an idea. True?"

He nodded. Beneath his shirt he quivered.

"I have no grand solution to your problems," I warned them. "What I have done is ponder a remark you made: that freedom lies in the unknown."

"Go on!" Leonce urged. She sat with fists clenched.

"Well," I said between puffs, "your latest account kind of reinforces my notion. That is, Wallis believes his organization, modified but basically the thing he founded, he believes it will be essential charge of the post-Maurai world. What you've discovered there doesn't make this seem any too plausible, hey? Ergo, somewhere, somewhen is an inconsistency. And . . . for what happened in between, you do merely have the word of Caleb Wallis, who is vainglorious and was born more than a hundred years ago."

"What's his birth got to do with the matter?" Havig demanded.

"Quite a bit," I said. "Ours has been a bitter century. Hard lessons have been learned which Wallis's generation never needed, never imagined. He may have heard about concepts like operations analysis, but he doesn't use them, they aren't in his marrow."

Havig tensed.

"Your chronolog gadget is an example of twentieth-century thinking," I continued. "By the way, what became of it?"

"The one I had got left in Pera when . . . when I was captured," he replied. "I imagine whoever acquired the house later threw it out or broke it apart for junk. Or maybe feared it might be magical and heaved it in the Horn. I've had new ones made."

A thrill passed through me, and I began to understand Leonce the huntress a little. "The men who took you, even a fairly sophisticated man like that Krasicki, did not think to bring it along for examination," I said. "Which illustrates my point nicely. Look, Jack, every time traveler hits the bloody nuisance of targeting on a desired moment. To you, it was a matter of course to consider the problem, decide what would solve it—an instrument—and find a company which was able to accept your commission to invent the thing for you."

I exhaled a blue plume. "It never occurred to Wallis," I finished. "To any of his gang. That approach doesn't come natural to them."

Silence descended anew.

"Well," Havig said, "I am the latest-born traveler they found prior to the Judgment."

"Uh-huh," I nodded. "Take advantage of that. You've

made a beginning, in your research beyond the Maurai period. It may seem incredible to you that Wallis's people haven't done the same kind of in-depth study. Remember, though, he's from a time when foresight was at a minimum—a time when everybody assumed logging and strip-mining could go on forever. It was the century of Clerk Maxwell, yes—I'm thinking mainly of his work on what we call cybernetics—and Babbage and Peirce and Ricardo and Clausewitz and a slew of other thinkers whom we're still living off of. But the seeds those minds were planting hadn't begun to sprout and flower. Anyhow, like many time travelers, it seems, Wallis didn't stay around to share the experiences of his birth era. No, he had to skate off and become the almighty superman.

"Jack, from the painfully gathered learning of the race, *you* can profit."

Leonce seemed puzzled. Well, my philosophy was new to her too. The man had grown altogether absorbed. "What do you propose?" he asked low.

"Nothing specifically," I answered. "Everything generally. Concentrate more on strategy than tactics. Don't try to campaign by your lone selves against an organization; no, start a better outfit."

"Where are the members coming from?"

"Everywhere and everywhen. Wallis showed a degree of imagination in his recruiting efforts, but his methods were crude, his outlook parochial. For instance, surely more travelers are present that day in Jerusalem. His agents latched onto those who were obvious, and quit. There must be ways to attract the notice of the rest."

"Well . . . m-m-m . . . I had been giving thought to that myself." Havig cupped his chin. "Like maybe passing through the streets, singing lines from the Greek mass—"

"And the Latin. You can't afford grudges." I gripped my pipe hard. "Another point. Why must you stay this secretive? Oh, yes, your 'uncle' self was right, as far as he went. A child revealed to be a time traveler would've been in a fairly horrible bind. But you're not a child any longer.

"Moreover, I gather, Wallis considers ordinary persons a lesser breed. He's labeled them 'commoners,' hasn't he? He keeps them in subordinate positions. All he's accomplished by that has been to wall their brains off from him.

"I've done a little quiet sounding out, at places like Holberg College and Berkeley. There *are* good, responsible scholars at Berkeley! I can name you men and women who'll accept the fact of what you are, and respect your confidence, and help you, same as me."

"For why?" Leonce wondered.

Havig sprang from his chair and stormed back and forth across the room as he gave her the blazing answer which had broken upon him: "To open the world, darlya! Our kind can't be born only in the West. That doesn't make sense. China, Japan, India, Africa, America before the white man came—we've got the whole of humanity to draw on! And we—" he stuttered in his eagerness—"we can leave the bad, take the good, find the young and, dammit, bring them up right. My God! Who cares about a wretched gang of bullies uptime? *We* can make the future!"

It was not that simple, of course. In fact, they spent more than ten years of their lifespans in preparing. True, these included their private concerns. When I saw them next (after his one telephone call), briefly in March, they behaved toward each other like any happily long-married couple. Nonetheless, that was a strenuous, perilous decade.

Even more was it a period which demanded the hardest thought and the subtlest realism. The gathering of Havig's host would have used every year that remained in his body, and still be incomplete, had he not gone about it along the lines I suggested. Through me he met those members of think tanks and faculties I had bespoken. After he convinced them, they in turn introduced him to chosen colleagues, until he had an exceedingly high-powered advisory team. (Several have later quit their careers, to go into different work or retirement. It puzzles their associates.) At intervals I heard about their progress. The methods they developed for making contact—through much of the history of much of the world—would fill a book. Most failed; but enough succeeded.

For example, a searcher looked around, inquired discreetly around, after people who seemed to have whatever kind of unusualness was logical for a traveler residing in the given milieu. A shaman, village witch, local monk with a record of helping those who appealed to him or her by especially practical miracles. A peasant who flourished because somehow he never planted or harvested so as to get caught by bad weather. A merchant who made correspondingly lucky investments in ships, when storms and pirates caused heavy attrition. A warrior who was an uncatchable spy or scout. A boy who was said to counsel his father. Once in a while, persons like these would turn out to be the real thing. . . . Then there were ways of attracting their heed, such as being a wandering fortune-teller of a peculiar sort. . . .

To the greatest extent possible, the earliest traveler recruits were trained into a cadre of recruiters, who wasted no energy in being uptime overlords. Thus the finding of folk could snowball. Here, too, methods were available beyond the purview of a nineteenth-century American who regarded the twentieth as decadent and every other culture as inferior. There are modern ways to get a new language into a mind fast. There are ancient ways, which the West has neglected, for developing body and senses. Under the lash of wars, revolutions, invasions, and occupations, we have learned how to form, discipline, protect, and use a band of brothers—systematically.

Above everything else, perhaps, was today's concept of working together. I don't mean its totaliarian version, for which Jack Havig had total loathing, or that "togetherness," be it in a corporation or a commune, which he despised. I mean an enlightened pragmatism that rejects self-appointed aristocrats, does not believe received doctrine is necessarily true, stands ready to hear and weigh what anyone has to offer, and maintains well-developed channels to carry all ideas to the leadership and back again.

Our age will go down in fire. But it will leave gifts for which a later mankind will be grateful.

Now finding time travelers was a barebones beginning. They had to be organized. How? Why should they want to leave home, accept restrictions, put their lives on the line? What would keep them when they grew tired or bored or fearful or lonesome for remembered loves?

The hope of fellowship with their own kind would draw many, of course. Havig could gain by that, as Wallis had done. It was insufficient, though. Wallis had a variety of further appeals. Given the resources of his group, a man saw the world brought in reach and hardly a limit put on atavistic forms of self-indulgence. To the intelligent, Wallis offered power, grandeur, a chance—a duty, if you let yourself be convinced, which is gruesomely easy to do—to become part of destiny.

Then there were those who wanted to learn, or be at the highest moments of mankind's achievement, or simply and honorably enjoy adventuring. To them Havig could promise a better deal.

But this would still not give motive to wage war on the Eyrie. Monstrous it might be, the average traveler would concede; yet most governments, most institutions have in their own ways been monstrous. What threat was the Sachem?

"Setting up indoctrination courses—" Havig sighed to me. "A nasty work, that, isn't it? Suggest browbeating and incessant propaganda. But honest, we just want to explain. We try to make the facts clear, so our recruits can see for themselves how the Eyrie is by its nature unable to leave them be. It's not easy. You got any ideas on how to show a samurai of the Kamakura Period that the will of anybody to rule the world, anybody whatsoever, is a direct menace to him? I'm here mainly to see what my anthropologists and semanticists have come up with. Meanwhile, well, okay, we've got other pitches too, like primitive loyalty to chief and comrades, or the fun of a good scrap, or . . . well, yes, the chance to get rich, in permissible ways. And, for the few, a particular dream—"

At that, I envied him the challenge of his task. Imagine: finding, and afterward forging mutuality between a Confucian teacher, a boomerang-wielding kangaroo hunter, a Polish schoolboy, a medieval Mesopotamian peasant, a West African ironsmith, a Mexican vaquero, an Eskimo girl. . . . The very effort to assemble that kaleidoscope may have been his greatest strength. Such people did not need to learn much about the Eyrie before they realized that, for most of them as time travelers, Havig's was the only game in town.

They got this preliminary training in scattered places and eras. Afterward they were screened for trustworthiness; the means were a weird and wonderful potpourri. The dubious cases—a minor percentage—were brought to their home locations, guided to their home years, paid off, and bidden farewell. They had not received enough information about the enemy to contact it; generally they lived thousands of miles away.

The majority were led to the main base, for further training and for the work of building it and its strength.

This was near where the Eyrie would be, but immensely far downtime, in the middle Pleistocene. That precaution created problems of its own. The temporal passage was lengthy for the traveler, requiring special equipment as well as intermediate resting places. Caches must be established en route, and everything ferried piece by piece, stage by slow stage. But the security was worth this, as was the stronghold itself. It stood on a wooded hill, and through the valley below ran a mighty river which Leonce told me shone in the sunlight like bronze.

The search methods had discovered members of both sexes in roughly equal numbers. Thus a community developed—kept childless, except for its youngest members, nevertheless a community which found an identity, laws and precedences and ceremonies and stories and mysteries, in a mere few years, and was bound together by its squabbles as well as its loves. And this was Havig's real triumph. The Sachem had created an army; the man sworn to cast him down created a tribe.

I heard these things when Havig and Leonce paid me that March visit. They were then in the midst of the work. Not till All Hallows' Eve did I learn the next part of their story.

chapter 15

The shadows which were time reeled past. They had form and color, weight and distances, only when one emerged for food or sleep or a hurried gulp of air. Season after season blew across the hills; glaciers from the north ground heights to plains and withdrew in a fury of snowstorms, leaving lakes where mastodon drank; the lakes thickened to swamps and finally to soil on whose grass fed horses and camels, whose treetops were grazed by giant sloths, until the glaciers returned; mild weather renewed saw those earlier beasts no more, but instead herds of bison which darkened the prairie and filled it with an earthquake drumroll of hoofs; the pioneers entered, coppery-skinned men who wielded flint-tipped spears; again was a Great Winter, again a Great Springtime, and now the hunters had bows, and in this cycle forest claimed the moraines, first willow and larch and scrub oak, later an endless cathedral magnificence—and suddenly that was gone, in a blink, the conquerors were there, grubbing out a million stumps which the axes had left, plowing and sowing, reaping and threshing, laying down trails of iron from which at night could be heard a rush and a long-drawn wail strangely like mastodon passing by.

Havig's group stopped for a last rest in the house of a young farmer who was no traveler but could be trusted. They needed it for a depot, too. It would have been impossible to go this far through time on this point of Earth's surface without miniature oxygen tanks. Otherwise, they'd more than once have had to stop for air when the country lay drowned, or been unable to because they were under a mile of ice. Those were strong barriers which guarded the secret of their main base from the Eyrie.

The equipment absorbed most of their mass-carrying ability. Here was a chance to get weapons.

Lantern light glowed mellow on an oilcloth-covered kitchen table, polished iron and copper, stove where wood crackled to keep warm a giant pot of coffee. Though the nearest neighbors were half an hour's horseback ride straight across the fields, and screened off by trees, Olav Torstad must always receive his visitors after dark. At that, he was considered odd for the occasional midnight gleam in his windows. But he was otherwise a steady fellow; most likely, the neighbors decided, now and then a bachelor would have trouble sleeping.

"You're already fixing to go again?" he asked.

"Yes," Havig said. "We've ground to cover before dawn, remember."

Torstad stared at Leonce. "Sure don't seem right, a lady bound for war."

"Where else but by her man?" she retorted. With a grin: "Jack couldn't talk me out of it either. Spare your breath."

"Well, different times, different ways," Torstad said, "but I'm glad I was born in 1850." In haste: "Not that I don't appreciate everything you've done for me."

"You've done more for us," Havig answered. "We grubstaked you to this place strictly because we needed something of the kind close to where the Eyrie will be. You assumed the ongoing risk, and the burden of keeping things hidden, and— No matter. Tonight it ends." He constructed a smile. "You can get rid of what stuff we leave behind, marry that girl you're engaged to, and live the rest of your days at peace."

For a few seconds, behind Torstad's eyes, something rattled its chains. "At peace?" Abruptly: "You will come back, won't you? Tell me what happened? Please!"

"If we win," Havig said, and thought how many such promises he had left, how many more his followers must have left, across the breadth and throughout the duration of the space-time they had roved. He jumped from his chair. "Come on, let's get the military gear for our men. If you'll hitch up a team, we'd like a wagon ride to the site. Let's move!"

Others were moving. They are. They will be.

It was no enormous host; it totaled perhaps three thousand. Some two-thirds were women, the very young, the old, the handicapped: time porters, nurses, whatever kind of noncombatants were required. But this was still too many to gather at one intermediate station, making rumors and traces which an enemy might come upon. Simply bringing them all to America had been an endlessly complex problem in logistics and secrecy.

Beneath huge trees, in a year before Columbus, some took a deer path. The Dakotan who guided them would have become the next medicine man of his tribe, had a patient wanderer not found him. The chronolog he carried, like other leaders elsewhere and elsewhen, would identify an exact place before he set it for an equally precise instant.

Once during the eighteenth century, certain *coureurs de bois* made rendezvous and struck off into the wilderness.

Not quite a hundred years after, the captain of a group

explained to what few white people he met that the government in Washington wished a detailed survey prior to establishing a territory.

Later it became common if unofficial knowledge that you saw Negroes hereabouts—briefly—because this was a station of the Underground Railway.

In the 1920's one did not question furtive movements and gatherings. It was common if unofficial knowledge that this was a favorite route for importers of Canadian whiskey.

Later an occasional bus marked CHARTERED passed through the area, setting off passengers and baggage in the middle of the night, then proceeding with its sign changed to NOT IN SERVICE.

Toward the close of the century, a jumbo jet lumbered aloft. The motley lot of humans aboard drew no special attention. "International Friendship Tours" were an almost everyday thing, as private organizations and subdivisions of practically every government snatched at any imaginable means to help halt the dream-dance down to catastrophe.

Well afterward, a fair-sized band of horsemen trotted through the region. Their faces and accouterments said they were Mong. The invaders never did establish themselves in these parts, so their early scouts were of no importance.

Havig and his half dozen flashed back into normal time.

His chronolog had winked red an hour before sunrise, on New Year's Day in the one hundred and seventy-seventh year of the Eyrie's continuous existence. The sky loomed darkling to the west, where stars and planets stood yet aglow, but ice-gray in the east. Shadowless light brought forth every brick of walls and keep and towers; it glimmered off window glass and whitened frost upon courtyard paving. Enormous stillness enclosed the world, as if all sound had frozen in that cold which bit lungs and smoked from nostrils.

This band had rehearsed what they must do often enough. Nonetheless his glance swept across them, these his troopers chosen for the heart of the mission.

They were dressed alike, in drab-green parkas, padded trousers tucked into leather boots, helmets and weapons and equipment-loaded belts. He knew their faces better, their very gaits, after lifespan years of comradeship: Leonce, ablaze with eagerness, a stray ruddy lock crossing the brow he had kissed; Chao, Indhlovu, Gutierrez, Bielawski, Maatuk ibn Nahal. For a pulsebeat their hands remained clasped together. Then they let go. He set down his chronolog. They readied their guns ere the sentries at the battlements should spy them and cry out.

The odds favored surprise. The hinterland was firmly controlled, had been for long years, would be for longer. Had not the Sachem verified this on his journeys to his future selves? More and more the Eyrie prospered, not alone in wealth but in recruits to serve the great purpose. So one could be at ease during a holiday. As many agents as possible took their furloughs in winter, to escape its gloom and cold. But the Sachem was always present for a New Year, whose eve began with ceremonies and speeches, ended with revelry. Who could blame a guard if, in the bitterness before dawn, eyes bleared and lids drooped?

"Okay," Havig said; "I love you, Leonce," he whispered. Her lips winged across his. The band loped to the door of that tower wherein dwelt Caleb Wallis.

It was immovable. The woman cursed: "—Oktai's tail, I didn' 'spec'—" Maatuk's .45 blasted out the lock. The noise smote eardrums, rang between the sleeping walls. A thought flashed through Havig. *No combat operation goes perfectly. My studies told me, always allow a margin—*

But this was the one part of the whole thing where slippage could most readily throw him off the cliff.

He led their way inside. Behind them, he heard a shout. Was it more puzzled than alarmed, or did he delude himself? Never mind. In the entryroom, up the stairs!

Soles clattered on stone. The impact jarred through Havig's shins, clear to his teeth. Four were at his back, leaping along a dusky skyward spiral. Gutierrez and Bielawski had taken station below, to guard main door and elevator exit. Indhlovu and Chao peeled off on the second and third levels, to capture the apartments of a secretary—Havig didn't know who he currently was—and Austin Caldwell. And here, next landing, brass-bound, here bulked the portal to Wallis.

That wasn't secured. Nobody dared enter uninvited, unless they came armed to bring this whole creation down. Havig flung the door wide.

Again he knew wainscoting, furriness, heavy desk and chairs, photographs of masters and mother. The air lay hot and damp. Frost blinded, windowpanes, making twilight within. Maatuk whirled about to keep the entrance. Havig and Leonce burst on into the suite beyond.

Wallis surged from a canopied double bed. Havig was flickeringly shocked at how the past several lifespan years had bitten the man. He was quite gray. The face was less red than netted in broken veinlets, and sagged beneath its weight. Horrible, somehow, because of being funny to see, was his nightshirt. He groped for a pistol on an end table.

"Ya-a-a-ah!" Leonce screamed, and launched herself in a flying leap.

Wallis vanished from sight. Likewise did she, her fingers upon him. They reappeared, rolling over and over across the floor, wrestling, he unable to flee through time while she gripped him and set her will to stay in the now. Their breath rasped through the shrieks of some commoner girl behind the bed draperies. Havig circled about, in search of a way to help. The grapplers were well matched, and desperate. He saw no opening which wasn't gone before he could strike.

Gunfire raged in the anteroom.

Havig pelted to the inner door, flattened himself, peered around the jamb. Maatuk sprawled moveless. Above him Austin Caldwell swayed, dripped blood, wheezed air through torn lungs, while his revolver wavered in search of more foemen. The old Indian fighter must have gotten the drop on Chao, or taken a couple of bullets and slain him anyway, as Maatuk had then been slain—

"You're covered! Surrender!" Havig called.

"Go . . . to . . . hell . . . traitor's hell. . . ." The Colt roared anew.

Across years Havig remembered many kindnesses and much grim swallowing of pain at what had seemed to be horrors inescapable in the service of the Sachem. He recalled his own followers, and Xenia. He slipped a minute uptime while he stepped into the doorway, emerged, and fired. His bullet clove air and shattered the glass on Charlemagne's photograph. Caldwell had crumpled.

Explosions racketed down in the yard, throughout keep and ancillary buildings. Havig hastened back to Leonce. She had gotten legs around Wallis' lower body and thumbs on his carotid arteries. He beat her about the shoulders, but she lowered her head and hung on. His blows turned feeble. They stopped.

"Make him fast," she panted. "Quick."

From a pocket Havig drew the set of manacles and chain which were standard equipment for every person of his. Squatting, he linked Wallis to the bedstead.

"He's not going anywhere," he said. "Unless somebody comes to release him. You stand guard against that."

She bridled. "An' miss the fun?"

"That's an order!" he snapped. She gave him a mutinous look but obeyed. Their whole plan turned on this prisoner. "I'll see about getting somebody to spell you, soon's may be," he said, adding: *When the battle's over.* He left. The concubine had fled, he noticed, and wondered briefly whether she was bereaved or relieved.

On the next level a balcony overlooked the courtyard. Here the Sachem delivered his speeches. Havig stepped forth, into waxing bleak light, and gazed across chaos. Fights raged between men and knots of men; wounded stirred and groaned, the slain looked shrunken where they lay. Yells and weapon-cracks insulted the sky.

There didn't seem to be a pattern to anything which happened, only ugliness. He unshipped a pair of binoculars and studied the scene more closely. They let him identify an occasional combatant. Or corpse . . . yes, Juan Mendoza yonder, and, O Christ, Jerry Jennings, whom he'd hoped could be saved—

A new squadron of his army blinked into normal time and deployed. And suddenly parachutes bloomed overhead, as those who had leaped out of a twentieth-century airplane, each with his chronolog, entered this day.

The confusion was more in seeming than truth. From the start, Wallis's on-duty garrison, most of them commoners, was nearly matched in numbers by a group of their traveler associates—who had been here for years and had quietly avoided drinking themselves befuddled last night. The fifth column was invented long before Havig was born; but his generation saw the unmerciful peak of its development and use.

Given it, and information carried forth by its members, and that precise timing which the chronolog made possible, and plans hammered out by a team which included professional soldiers, tested and rehearsed over and over on a mockup of the Eyrie itself . . . given this, Havig's victory was inevitable.

What counted was to minimize the number of agents who, seeing their disaster, would escape before they could be killed or secured. Of secondary importance in theory, but equal in Havig's breast, was to minimize casualties. On both sides.

He let the binoculars dangle loose, took a walkie-talkie radio off his shoulder, and began calling his squadron leaders.

"Between surprise and efficiency," he told me, "we didn't lose many who time-hopped. Some of those we collared 'later.' Knowing from the registers who they were, we could make fairly good guesses at where-when they'd headed for. It wouldn't be a random flight, you see. A man would have to seek a milieu where he might survive by himself. That didn't give too wide a choice."

"You didn't net the entire lot?" I fretted.

"No, not quite. We could scarcely hope for that."

"I should think even one, prowling loose, is too many. He can slip back uptime, though pastward of your attack, and warn—"

"That never worried me, Doc. I knew nobody ever has, therefore nobody ever will. Not that that can't be explained in ordinary human terms, quite apart from physics or metaphysics.

"Look, these were none of them supermen. In fact, they were either weaklings who'd been assigned civilian-type jobs, or warriors as ignorant and superstitious as brutal. Aside from what specialized training fitted them for Wallis's purposes, he'd never tried to get them properly educated. If nothing else, that might have led to questioning of his righteousness and infallibility.

"Therefore, those who did escape had their morale

pretty well shattered. Their main concern must be to stay hidden from us. And if they thought about the possibility of returning, they'd realize that we'd have agents of our own planted throughout the period of Wallis's reign, just a few but enough to keep a lookout for them and hustle them away before any warning could be delivered." Havig chuckled. "I was surprised myself, when first I learned who some of those people would be. Reuel Orrick, the old carnival charlatan . . . Boris, the monk who went to Jerusalem. . . ."

He paused for a drink of my scotch. "No," he finished, "we simply didn't want bandits loose who're able to skip clear of their crimes. And I think—I dare hope—that never happened. How can, say, a *condottiere*, penniless, educationless, entirely alone, how can he get along in any era of white America or make his way to Europe? No, really, his best bet is to seek out the Indians. And among them he can do better as a medicine man than a robber. He might actually end his days a useful member of the tribe! That's a single example, of course, but I imagine you get the general idea."

"Regardin' the future," Leonce said, her tone tiger-soft, "we hold that. The Eyrie for the years it has left; the Phase Two complex till it's no longer needed—an' *we* built it. We've learned from our campaign. Nobody will shake us loose."

"Well, in a military sense," her husband was quick to put in. "It can't be done overnight, but we mean to raise the Eyrie's subjects out of peonage, make them into a free yeomanry. Phase Two never will have subjects: instead, nontraveler members of our society. And—goes without saying, our agents behave themselves. They visit the past for nothing except research and recruitment. When they need an economic base for operations, they make it by trade which gives value for value."

Leonce stroked fingers across his cheek. "Jack comes from a sentimental era," she crooned.

I frowned in an effort to understand. "Wait a minute," I protested. "You had one huge problem with spines and fangs, right after you took the Eyrie. Your prisoners. What about them?"

An old trouble crossed Havig's countenance. "There was no good answer," he said tonelessly. "We couldn't release them, nor those we arrested as they came back from furlough or surprised in their fiefs. We couldn't gun them down. I mean that in a literal sense; we couldn't. Our whole force was drawn from people who had a conscience, able to learn humaneness if they hadn't been brought up with it. Nor did we want to keep anybody chained for life in some secret dungeon."

Leonce grinned. "Worse'n shootin', that," she said.

"Well," Havig plodded on, "you may remember—I think I told you, and the telling is closer to your present than it is to mine—about those psychodrugs they have in the late Maurai era. Do you recall? My friend Carelo Keajimu will be afraid of them, they give such power. Inject a person, talk to him while he's under the influence, and he'll believe whatever you order him to believe. Absolutely. Not fanatically, but in an 'of course' way that's far more deeply rooted. His own mind will supply rationalizations and false memories to explain contradictions. You see what this is? The ultimate brainwash! So complete that the victim never even guesses there ever was anything else."

I whistled. "Good Lord! You mean you converted those crooks and butcher boys to your side, en masse?"

Havig shuddered. "No. If nothing else, I at least could never have stood such a gang of, zombies. It'd have been necessary to wipe their entire past lives, and— Impractical, anyhow. Keajimu had arranged for several of my bright lads to be trained in psychotechnology, but their job was quite big enough already."

He drew breath, as if gathering courage, before he proceeded: "What we destroyed in our prisoners was their belief in time travel. We brought them to their home milieus—that took a lot of effort by itself, you realize—and treated them. They were told they'd had fever, or demonic possession, or whatever was appropriate; they'd imagined uncanny things which, being totally impossible, must never be mentioned and best never thought about; now they were well and should return to their ordinary lives.

"Our men released them and came back for more."

I pondered. "Well," I said, "I admit finding the idea a bit repulsive myself. But not too much. I've been forced to do certain things, tell certain lies, to patients and—"

Leonce stated: "There were two exceptions, Doc."

"Come with me," the mind molder said. His voice was gentle. Drug-numbed, Caleb Wallis clung to his hand as he left.

Havig remained, often toiling twice around the same clock, till he and his lieutenants had properly underway the immense task of making over the Eyrie. But time flowed, time flowed. At last he had no escape from the moment when the psychotechnician told him he could enter that guarded tower.

Perhaps the most appalling thing was how well the Sachem looked, how jauntily he sat behind his desk in an office from which scars and bloodstains were blotted as if they had never been.

"Well!" he greeted. "Good day, my boy, good day! Sit down. No, pour for us first. You know what I like."

Havig obeyed. The small eyes peered shrewdly at him. "Turned out to be a mighty long, tough mission, yours, hey?" Wallis said. "You've aged; you have. I'm sure glad you carried it off, though. Haven't read your full report, but I intend to. Meanwhile, let's catch up with each other." His glass lifted. "To the very good health of us both."

Havig forced down a sip and lowered himself to a chair.

"You've doubtless heard already, mine hasn't been the best," Wallis continued. "Down and out for quite a while. Actual brain fever. Some damn germ from past or future, probably. The sawbones claims germs have evolution like animals. I've about decided we should curtail our explorations, partly on that account, partly to concentrate on building up our power in normal time. What d' you think of that?"

"I think it would be wise, sir," Havig whispered.

"Another reason for pulling in our horns is, we lost a lot of our best men while you were away. Run of bad luck for us. Austin Caldwell, have you heard? And Waclaw Krasicki— Hey, you're white's a ghost! What's wrong? Sure you're okay?"

"Yes, sir. . . . Still tired. I did spend a number of years downtime, and—"

—and it had been Leonce who found Krasicki chained, said, "Xenia," drew her pistol and shot him in the head. But it was Havig who could not make himself be sorry this had happened, until Xenia sought him in his sleep and wept because he did not forgive.

Well. "I'll recover, sir."

"Fine. Fine. We need men like you." Wallis rubbed his brow. For a minute his voice came high and puzzled: "So many people here. So many old gone—or are they? I can't tell. I look from my balcony and see strangers, and think I ought to see, oh, somebody named Juan, somebody named Hans . . . many, many . . . but I can't place them. Did I dream them while I lay sick?" He hugged himself, as if winter air had seeped through into the tropical warmth around him. "Often, these days, I feel alone, in all space and time—"

Havig mustered briskness: "What you need, sir, if I may suggest it, is an extended vacation. I can recommend places."

"Yes, I think you're right. I do." Wallis gulped from his tumbler and fumbled after a cigar.

"When you return, sir," Havig said, "you ought to work less hard. The foundation has been laid. We're functioning smoothly."

"I know. I know." Wallis lost hold of his match.

"What we need, sir, is not your day-by-day instruction any longer. We have plenty of competent men to handle details. We need more your broad overview, the basic direction you foresee—your genius."

Behind the gray whiskers, Wallis simpered. This time he got his cigar lit.

"I've been talking about it with various officers, and thinking a lot, too," Havig proceeded. "They've discussed the matter with you, they said. Sir, let me add my words to theirs. We believe the ideal would be if a kind of schedule was established for your passage through the future. Of course, it'd include those periods your past self will visit, to let you show him how well everything is going. Otherwise, however—uh—we don't think you should spend more than a minimum of your lifespan in any single continuous set of dates. You're too precious to the grand project."

"Yes. I'd about decided the same for myself." Wallis nodded and nodded. "First, like you say, a real good vacation, to straighten out my thoughts and get this fuzziness out of my head. Then, a . . . a progress through tomorrow, observing, issuing orders, always bound onward . . . till at the end, when my work is done— Yes. Yes. Yes."

* * *

"God!" I exclaimed, a word as close to prayer as I'd come in fifty skeptical years. "If ever there was a revenge—"

"This wasn't," Havig said though lips drawn taut.

"What, well, what'd it feel like, when he came?"

"I've avoided being on hand for most of that. When I had to be, it was naturally always a festive occasion, and nobody cared if I got drunk. Men who regularly deal with him told me—tell me—one gets used to leading the poor apparition through his Potemkin villages, and off to some sybaritic place downtime for one of the long orgiastic celebrations which use up and shorten his lifespan. They're almost fond of him. They go to great lengths to put on a good show. That eases their thought of the end."

"Huh? Isn't he supposed to vanish in his old age?"

Havig's fist knotted on the arm of his chair. "He did. He will. He'll scream in the night, and his room will be empty. He must have thrown himself far in time, because searchers up and down will find nothing reappearing." Havig tossed off his drink. I saw he needed more, and obliged.

Leonce caressed him. "Aw, don't let it gnaw you, darlya," she murmured. "He's not worth that."

"Mostly I don't," he said, rough-throated. "Rather not discuss the business."

"I, I don't see—" I couldn't help stammering.

The big woman turned to me. She smiled in tenderness for her vulnerable man. What she said was, to her, a remark of no importance: "We been told, now an' then as it's dyin' a brain throws off the effect o' that drug an' recalls what was real."

chapter 16

In 1971, October 31 fell on a Sunday. That meant school next day. The little spooks would come thick and fast to my door if they must be early abed. I laid in ample supplies. When I was a boy, Halloween gave license for limited hell-raising, but I'm glad the custom has softened. Seeing them in their costumes brings back my own children at that same age, and Kate. When my doorbell has rung for the last time, I usually make a fire, settle with my favorite pipe and a mug of hot cider, maybe put some music she liked on the record player, look into the flames and remember. In a quiet way I am happy.

But this day called me forth. It was cool, noisy with wind, sunshine spilling through diamond-clear air, and the trees stood scarlet, yellow, bronze, in enormous tossing rustling masses against blueness where white clouds scudded, and from a V passing high overhead drifted down a trumpet song. I went for a hike.

On the sidewalks of Senlac, leaves capered before me, making sounds like laughter at the householders who tried to rake them into neat piles. The fields outside of town stretched bare and dark and waiting; but flocks of crows still gleaned them, until rising in a whirl of wings and raucous merriment. I left the paved county road for an old dirt one which cars don't use much, thanks be to whatever godling loves us enough to wage his rearguard fight against this kind of Progress. In its roundabout fashion it also brought me to Morgan Woods.

I went through that delirium of color till I reached the creek. There I stood a while on the bridge, watching water gurgle above stones, a squirrel assert his dominion over an oak which must be a century old, branches toss, leaves tear loose; I listened to the rush and skirl and deeper tones around me, felt air slide by like chilly liquid, drew in odors of damp and fulfillment; I didn't think about anything in particular, or contemplate, or meditate, I just was there.

At last my bones and thin flesh reminded me they had a goodly ways to go, and I started home. Tea and scones seemed an excellent idea. Afterward I should write Bill and Judy a letter, make specific proposals about my visit to them this winter in California. . . .

I didn't notice the car parked under the chestnut tree before I was almost upon it. Then my pulse jumped inside me. Could this be—? Not the same machine as before, but of course he always rented— I forgot whatever ache was in my legs and trotted forward.

Jack and Leonce Havig sprang forth to greet me. We embraced, the three of us in a ring. "Welcome, welcome!" I babbled. "Why didn't you call ahead? I'd not've kept you waiting."

"That's okay, Doc," he answered. "We've been sitting and enjoying the scene." He was mute for a second or two. "We're taking in as much of Earth as we're able."

I stepped back and considered him. He was leaner than before, deep furrows beside his mouth and between his eyes, the skin sun-touched but leather-dry, the blond hair fading toward gray. Middle forties, I judged; something like a decade had gone through him in the weeks of mine since last we met. . . . I turned to his wife. Erect, lithe, more full-figured than earlier but carrying it well, she showed the passage of those years less than he did. To be sure, I thought, she was younger. Yet I marked crow's-feet wrinkles and the tiny frost-flecks in that red mane.

"You're done?" I asked, and shivered with something else than the weather. "You beat the Eyrie?"

"We did, we did," Leonce jubilated. Havig merely nodded. A starkness had entered the alloy of him. He kept an arm around her waist, however, and I didn't suppose she could stay happy if at heart he were not too.

"Wonderful!" I cried. "Come on in."

"For tea?" she laughed.

"Lord, no! I had that in mind, but—my dear, this calls for Aalborg akvavit and Carlsberg beer, followed by Glenlivet and— Well, I'll phone Swanson's and have 'em deliver gourmet items and we'll fix the right breed of supper and— How long can you stay?"

"Not very long, I'm afraid," Havig said. "A day or two at most. We've a lot to do in the rest of our lifespans."

Their tale was hours in the telling. Sunset flared gold and hot orange across a greenish western heaven, beyond trees and neighbor roofs, when I had been given the skeleton of it. The wind had dropped to a mumble at my threshold. Though the room was warm enough, I felt we could use a fire and bestirred myself to fill the hearth. But Leonce said, "Let me." Her hands had not lost their woodcraft, and she remained a pleasure to watch. Pleasure it was, also, after the terrible things I had heard, to see how his gaze followed her around.

"Too bad you can't forestall the founding of the Eyrie," I said.

"We can't, and that's that," Havig replied. Slowly: "I'm not sure it is too bad, either. Would a person like me ever have had the . . . determination? I started out hoping for no more than to meet my fellows. Why should I have wanted to organize them for any special purpose, until—" His voice trailed off.

"Xenia," I murmured. "Yes."

Leonce glanced around at us. "Even Xenia doesn't tip the balance," she said in a gentle tone. "The Crusaders would not've spared her. As was, she got rescued and lived nine years onward." She smiled. "Five of them were with Jack. Oh, she had far less than luck's given me, but she did have that."

I thought how Leonce was outwardly changed less than her man, and inwardly more than I had guessed.

While Havig made no remark, I knew his wound must have healed—scarred over, no doubt, but nonetheless healed—as wounds do in every healthy body and spirit.

"Well," I said, trying to break free of somberness, "you did get your kind together, you did overcome the wrong and establish the right. Well, I hardly expected I'd entertain a king and queen!"

"What?" Havig blinked in surprise. "We aren't."

"Eh? You rule the roost uptime, don't you?"

"No. For a while we did, because somebody had to. But we worked together with the wisest people we could find—not exclusively travelers by any means—to end this as soon as might be, and turn the military society into a free republic . . . and at last into nothing more than a sort of loose guild."

Fire, springing aloft when she worked the bellows, cast gleams from Leonce's eyes. "Into nothin' less than a dream," she said.

"I don't understand," I told them, as frequently this day.

Havig sought words. "Doc," he said after a bit, "once we've left here, you won't see us again."

I sat quite quietly. Sunset in the windows was giving way to dusk.

Leonce sped to me, cast arms around my shoulders, kissed my cheek. Her hair was fragrant, with a touch of smokiness from the little chuckling flames. "No, Doc," she said. "Not 'cause you'll die soon."

"I don't want—" I began.

"Ay-yeh." Barbarian bluntness spoke. "You said you don't want to know the date on your tombstone. An' we're not about to tell you, either. But damn, I will say you're good for a fair while yet!"

"The thing is," Havig explained in his awkward fashion, "we, Leonce and I, we'll be leaving Earth. I doubt we'll come back."

"What was the good of time travel, ever?" he demanded when we could discourse of fundamentals.

"Why, well, uh—" I floundered.

"To control history? You can't believe a handful of travelers would be able to do that. Wallis believed it, but you can't, I'm certain. Nor do you believe they should."

"Well . . . history, archeology—science—"

"Agreed, almost, that there's no such thing as too much knowledge. Except that fate ought not to be foreknown. That's the death of hope. And learning is an esthetic experience—or ecstatic—but if we stop there, aren't we being flat-out selfish? Don't you feel knowledge should be *used*?"

"Depends on the end, Jack."

Leonce, seated beside him, stirred in the yellow glow of a single shaded lamp, the shadow-restless many-hued sparkle from my fireplace. "For us," she said, "the end is goin' to the stars. That's what time travel is good for."

Havig smiled. His manner was restrained, but the same eagerness vibrated: "Why did you imagine we went on to build the—Phase Two complex—what we ourselves call Polaris House? I told you we don't care to rule the world. No, Polaris House is for research and development. Its work will be done when the first ships are ready."

"An' they will be," Leonce lilted. "We've seen."

Passion mounted in Havig. He leaned forward, fingers clenched around the glass he had forgotten he grasped, and said:

"I haven't yet mastered the scientific or engineering details. That's one reason we must go back uptime. Physicists talk about a mathematical equivalence between traveling into the past and flying faster than light. They hope to develop a theory which'll show them a method. Maybe they'll succeed, maybe they won't. I know they won't in Polaris House, but maybe at last, in Earth's distant future or on a planet circling another sun. But it doesn't ultimately matter. A ship can go slower than light if people like us are the crew. You follow me? Her voyage might last centuries. But to us, moving uptime while she moves across space, it's hours or minutes.

"Our children can't do the same. But they'll be *there*. We'll have started man on his way to infinity."

I stared past him. In the windows, the constellations were hidden by flamelight. "I see," I answered softly. "A tremendous vision for sure."

"A necessary one," Havig replied. "And without us—and thus, in the long view, without our great enemy—the thing would never have been done. The Maurai might've gathered the resources to revive space exploration, at the height of their power. But they did not. Their ban on enormous energy outlays was good at first, yes, vital to saving this planet. At last, though, like most good things, it became a fetish. . . . Undoubtedly the culture which followed them would not have gone to space."

"We did," Leonce exulted. "The Star Masters are our people."

"And a lifebringer to Earth," Havig added. "I mean, a civilization which just sat down and stared at its own inwardness—how soon would it become stagnant, caste-ridden, poor, and nasty? You can't think unless you have something to think about. And this has to come from outside. Doesn't it? The universe is immeasurably larger than any mind."

"I've gathered," I said, my words covering awe, "that the future society welcomes the starfarers."

"Oh, yes, oh, yes. More for their ideas than for material goods. Ideas, arts, experience, insights born on a thousand different worlds, out of a thousand different kinds of being—and Earth gives a fair return. It is well to have those mystics and philosophers. They think and feel, they search out meanings, they ask disturbing questions—" Havig's voice lifted. "I don't know where the communion between them and us will lead. Maybe to a higher state of the soul? I do believe the end will be good, and this is the purpose we time travelers are born for."

Leonce brought us partway back to our bodies. "Mainly," she laughed, "we 'spec' to have a hooraw o' fun. Climb down off your prophetic broomstick, Jack, honeybee, an' pay attention to your drink."

"You two intend, then, to be among the early explorers?" I asked redundantly.

"We've earned the right," she said.

"Uh—pardon me, none of my business, but if your children cannot inherit your gift—"

Wistfulness touched her. "Maybe we'll find a New Earth to raise them on. We're not too old." She regarded her man's sharp-edged profile. "Or maybe we'll wander the universe till we die. That'd be enough."

Silence fell. The clock on my mantel ticked aloud and the wind outside flowed past like a river.

The doorbell pealed. I left my chair to open up for a glimpse of Aquila. Three small figures were on the stoop, a clown, a bear, an astronaut. They held out paper bags. "Trick or treat!" they chanted. "Trick or treat!"

A year has fled since Jack Havig and Leonce of Wahorn bade me farewell. I often think about them. Mostly, of course, dailiness fills my days. But I often find an hour to think about them.

At any moment they may be somewhere on our planet, desperate or triumphant in that saga I already know. But we will not meet. The end of their lives reaches untellably far beyond mine.

Well, so does the life of man. Of Earth and the cosmos.

I wish . . . I wish many things. That they'd felt free to spend part of their stay in this summer which is past. We could have gone sailing. However, they naturally wanted to see Eleanor, his mother, in one of the few intervals they had been able to make sure were safe, and tell her—what? She has not told me.

I wish they or I had thought to raise a question which has lately haunted me.

How did the race of time travelers come to be?

We supposed, the three of us, that we knew the "why." But we did not ask who, or what, felt the need and responded.

Meaningless accidental mutation? Then curious that none like Havig seemed to have been born futureward of the Eyrie—of, anyhow, Polaris House. In truth it would probably not be good to have them and their foreknowledge about, once the purpose has been served of freeing man to roam and discover forever. But who decided this? Who shaped the reality?

I have been reading about recent work in experimental genetics. Apparently a virus can be made to carry genes from one host to the next; and the hosts need not be of the same species. Nature may have done this already, may always be doing it. Quite likely we bear in our cells and bequeath to our children bits of heritage from animals which were never among our forebears. That is well, if true. I am glad to think we may be so close to the whole living world.

But could a virus have been made which carried a very strange thing; and could it have been sown through a chosen part of the past by travelers created anew in some unimaginably remote tomorrow?

I walk beyond town, many of these nights, to stand under the high autumnal stars, look upward and wonder.